FIVE FEET APART

FIVE FEET APART

Rachael Lippincott
with Mikki Daughtry and Tobias Iaconis

SIMON & SCHUSTER

First published in Great Britain in 2019 by Simon & Schuster UK Ltd

First published in the USA in 2018 by Simon & Schuster BFYR, an imprint of Simon & Schuster Inc

3 5 7 9 10 8 6 4 2

Simon & Schuster UK Ltd
1st Floor, 222 Gray's Inn Road
London WC1X 8HB

www.simonandschuster.co.uk
www.simonandschuster.com.au
www.simonandschuster.co.in

Simon & Schuster Australia, Sydney
Simon & Schuster India, New Delhi

A CIP catalogue record for this book is available from the British Library.

PB ISBN 978-1-4711-8553-3
eBook ISBN 978-1-4711-8232-7

Printed and bound by CPI Group (UK) Ltd, Croydon, CR0 4YY

For Alyson

—R. L.

We dedicate this book, and the movie, to all the patients, families, medical staff, and loved ones who bravely fight the battle against cystic fibrosis every day. We hope the story of Stella and Will helps to bring awareness to this disease and, one day, a cure.

—M. D. and T. I.

CHAPTER 1

STELLA

I trace the outline of my sister's drawing, lungs molded from a sea of flowers. Petals burst out from every edge of the twin ovals in soft pinks, deep whites, even heather blues, but somehow each one has a uniqueness, a vibrancy that feels like it'll bloom forever. Some of the flowers haven't blossomed yet, and I can feel the promise of life just waiting to unfold from the tiny buds under the weight of my finger. Those are my favorites.

I wonder, all too often, what it would be like to have lungs this healthy. This *alive.* I take a deep breath, feeling the air fight its way in and out of my body.

Slipping off the last petal of the last flower, my hand sinks, fingers dragging through the background of stars, each pinpoint of light that Abby drew a separate attempt to capture infinity. I clear my throat, pulling my hand away, and lean over to grab a picture of us from off my bed. Identical smiles peek out from underneath thick wool scarves, the holiday lights at the park down the street twinkling above our heads just like the stars in her drawing.

There was something magical about it. The soft glow of the lampposts in the park, the white snow clinging to the branches of the trees, the quiet stillness of it all. We nearly froze our butts off for that picture last year, but it was our tradition. Me and Abby, braving the cold to go see the holiday lights together.

This photo always makes me remember that feeling. The feeling of going on an adventure with my sister, just the two of us, the world expanding like an open book.

I take a thumbtack and hang the picture next to the drawing before sitting down on my bed and grabbing my pocket notebook and pencil off my bedside table. My eyes travel down the long to-do list I made for myself this morning, starting with "#1: Plan to-do list," which I've already put a satisfying line through, and going all the way down to "#22: Contemplate the afterlife."

Number 22 was probably just a little ambitious for a Friday afternoon, but at least for now I can cross off number 17, "Decorate walls." I look around the formerly stark room I've spent the better part of the morning making my own, once again, the walls now filled with the artwork Abby's given me through the years, bits of color and life jumping out from clinical white walls, each one a product of a different trip to the hospital.

Me with an IV drip in my arm, the bag bursting with butterflies of different shapes and colors and sizes. Me wearing a nose cannula, the cable twisting to form an infinity sign. Me with my nebulizer, the vapor pouring out of it forming a cloudy halo. Then there's the most delicate one, a faded tornado of stars that she drew my very first time here.

It's not as polished as her later stuff, but somehow that makes me like it more.

And right underneath all that vibrancy is . . . my pile of medical equipment, sitting right next to a hideous green faux-leather hospital chair that comes standard for every room here at Saint Grace's. I eye the empty IV pole warily, knowing my first of many rounds of antibiotics over the next month is exactly an hour and nine minutes away. Lucky me.

"*Here it is!*" a voice calls from just outside my room. I look up as the door slowly creaks open and two familiar faces appear in the small crack of the doorway. Camila and Mya have visited me here a million times in the past decade, and they still can't get from the lobby to my room without asking every person in the building for directions.

"Wrong room," I say, grinning as a look of pure relief washes over them.

Mya laughs, pushing the door open the rest of the way. "It honestly could've been. This place is still a freaking maze."

"Are you guys excited?" I say, hopping up to give them both hugs.

Camila pulls away to look at me, pouting, her dark-brown hair practically drooping along with her. "Second trip in a row without you."

It's true. This isn't the first time my cystic fibrosis has taken me out of the running for some class trip or sunny vacation or school event. About 70 percent of the time, things are pretty normal for me. I go to school, I hang out with Camila and Mya, I work on my app. I just do it all with low-functioning lungs. But for the remaining 30 percent of my time, CF controls my life. Meaning when I need to return to the hospital for a tune-up, I miss out on things like a class trip to the art museum or now our senior trip to Cabo.

This particular tune-up just happens to be centered around the fact that I need to be pumped with antibiotics to finally get rid of a sore throat and a fever that won't go away.

That, and my lung function is tanking.

Mya plunks down on my bed, sighing dramatically as she lies back. "It's only two weeks. Are you sure you can't come? It's our *senior trip*, Stella!"

"I'm sure," I say firmly, and they know I mean it. We've been friends since middle school, and they know by now that when it comes to plans, my CF gets the final say.

It's not like I don't want to go. It's just, quite literally, a matter of life or death. I can't go off to Cabo, or anywhere for that matter, and risk not coming back. I can't do that to my parents. Not now.

"You were the head of the planning committee this year, though! Can't you get them to move your treatments? We don't want you to be stuck here," Camila says, gesturing to the hospital room I so carefully decorated.

I shake my head. "We still have spring break together! And I haven't missed a spring break 'Besties Weekend' since eighth grade, when I got that cold!" I say, smiling hopefully and looking back and forth between Camila and Mya. Neither of them returns my smile, though, and both opt to continue looking like I killed their family pets.

I notice they're both holding the bags of bathing suits I told them to bring, so I grab Camila's out of her hand in a desperate attempt to change the subject. "Ooh, suit options! We have to pick out the best ones!" Since I'm not going to be basking in the warm Cabo sun in a bathing suit of my choice, I figure I can at least live a little vicariously through my friends by picking out theirs with them.

This perks them both up. We eagerly dump their bags out on my bed, creating a mishmash of florals and polka dots and fluorescents.

I scan Camila's pile of bathing suits, grabbing a red one that falls somewhere between a bikini bottom and a single piece of thread, which I know without a doubt is a hand-me-down from her older sister, Megan.

I toss it to her. "This one. It's very you."

Her eyes widen, and she holds it up to her waist, fixing her wire-frame glasses in surprise. "I mean, the tan lines would be pretty great—"

"Camila," I say, grabbing a white-and-blue-striped bikini that I can tell will fit her like a glove. "I'm kidding. This one's perfect."

She looks relieved, grabbing the bikini from me. I turn my attention to Mya's pile, but she's busy texting away from the green hospital chair in the corner, a big smile plastered on her face.

I dig out a one-piece that she's had since swim class in sixth grade, holding it up to her with a smirk. "How's this, Mya?"

"Love it! Looks great!" she says, typing furiously.

Camila snorts, putting her suits back in the bag and giving me a sly smile. "Mason and Brooke called it quits," she says in explanation.

"Oh my god. They did not!" I say. This is news. *Amazing* news.

Well, not for Brooke. But Mya has been crushing on Mason since Mrs. Wilson's English class sophomore year, so this trip is her chance to finally make a move.

It bums me out I won't be there to help her make a killer ten-step "Whirlwind Cabo Romance with Mason" plan.

Mya puts her phone away and shrugs casually, standing and pretending to look at some of the artwork on the walls. "No big deal. We're going to meet him and Taylor at the airport tomorrow morning."

I give her a look and she breaks out into a huge smile. “Okay, it’s a little bit of a big deal!”

We all squeal with excitement, and I hold up an adorable polka-dot one-piece that is super vintage, and right up her alley. She nods, grabbing it and holding it up to her body. “I was *totally* hoping you’d pick this one.”

I look over to see Camila glancing at her watch nervously, which is no surprise. She’s a champion procrastinator and probably hasn’t packed a single thing for Cabo yet.

Besides the bikini, of course.

She sees me notice her checking her watch and grins sheepishly. “I still need to buy a beach towel for tomorrow.”

Classic Camila.

I stand up, my heart sinking in my chest at the thought of them leaving, but I don’t want to hold them up. “You guys have to get going, then! Your plane is at, like, the ass crack of dawn tomorrow.”

Mya looks around the room sadly while Camila twists her bag of suits dejectedly around her hand. The two of them are making this even harder than I thought it would be. I swallow the guilt and annoyance that come bubbling up. It’s not like they’re the ones missing their senior trip to Cabo. At least they’ll be together.

I give them both big smiles, practically pulling them to the door with me. My cheeks hurt from all this fake positivity, but I don’t want to ruin it for them.

"We'll send you a bunch of pictures, okay?" Camila says, giving me a hug.

"You'd better! Photoshop me into a few," I say to Mya, who is a wizard at Adobe. "You won't even know I wasn't there!"

They linger in the doorway, and I give them an exaggerated eye roll, playfully shoving them out into the hallway. "Get outta here. Go have a great trip."

"Love you, Stella!" they call as they walk down the hallway. I watch them go, waving until Mya's bouncing curls are completely out of sight, suddenly wanting nothing more than to be walking out with them, off to pack instead of unpack.

My smile fades as I close the door and see the old family picture pinned carefully to the back of my door.

It was taken a few summers ago on the front porch of our house during a Fourth of July barbecue. Me, Abby, Mom, and Dad, goofy smiles on all our faces as the camera captures the moment. I feel a swell of homesickness as I hear the sound of the worn, rickety wood of that front step, creaking underneath us as we laugh and get close for the picture. I miss that feeling. All of us together, happy and healthy. For the most part.

This isn't helping. Sighing, I pull myself away, looking over at the medicine cart.

In all honesty, I like it here. It's been my home away from home since I was six, so I usually don't mind coming. I get my treatments, I take my medicine, I drink my body weight in milk shakes, I get to see Barb and Julie, I leave until my next flare-up. Simple as that. But this time I feel anxious, restless even. Because instead of just wanting to get healthy, I *need* to get healthy. For my parents' sake.

Because they've gone and messed up everything by getting divorced. And after losing each other, they won't be able to handle losing me, too. I know it.

If I can get better, maybe . . .

One step at a time. I head over to the wall oxygen, double-checking the flowmeter is set properly, and listen for the steady hiss of the oxygen coming out of it before I pull the tube around my ears and slide the prongs of the cannula into my nose. Sighing, I sink down onto the familiarly uncomfortable hospital mattress, and take a deep breath.

I reach for my pocket notebook to read the next thing on my to-do list and keep myself preoccupied—"#18: Record a video."

I grab my pencil and bite it thoughtfully as I stare at the words I wrote earlier. Oddly enough, contemplating the afterlife seems easier right now.

But the list is the list, so, exhaling, I reach over to my bedside table to get my laptop, sitting cross-legged on the new floral comforter I picked out yesterday at Target while Camila and Mya were buying clothes for Cabo. I didn't even need the comforter, but they were so enthusiastic in helping me pick something out for my trip to the hospital, I felt bad not getting it. At least it sort of matches my walls now, bright and vibrant and colorful.

I drum my fingers anxiously on the keyboard, and squint at my reflection in the screen while my computer starts up. I frown at the mess of long brown hair and try to smooth it down, running my fingers through it over and over. Frustrated, I pull my hair tie off my wrist and resort to a messy bun in an attempt to look halfway decent for this video. I grab my copy of *Java Coding for Android Phones* off my bedside table and put my laptop on top of it, so I don't show some serious under chin, and can have a shot that's remotely flattering.

Logging on to my YouTube Live account, I adjust the webcam, making sure you can see Abby's lung drawing directly behind me.

It's the perfect backdrop.

I close my eyes and take a deep breath, hearing the familiar wheeze of my lungs trying desperately to fill with air through the sea of mucus. Exhaling slowly, I slap a big Hallmark-greeting-card smile on my face before opening my eyes and pressing the enter key to go live.

"Hey, guys. Is everyone having a good Black Friday? I waited for snow that never came!"

I glance into the corner of my screen as I turn the camera toward the hospital window, the sky a cloudy gray, the trees on the other side of the glass completely barren. I smile as my livestream count goes steadily past 1K, a fraction of the

23,940 YouTube subscribers who tune in to see how my battle with cystic fibrosis is going.

"So, I could be getting ready to go on a plane to Cabo for my school's senior trip, but instead I'll be spending this holiday at my home away from home, thanks to a mild sore throat."

Plus, a raging fever. I think back to when I got my temperature taken on intake this morning, the flashing numbers on the thermometer blaring out a strong 102. I don't want to mention it in the video, though, because my parents will definitely be watching this later.

As far as they know, I just have a nagging cold.

"Who needs two whole weeks of sunshine and blue skies and beaches when you can have a month of luxury right in your own backyard?"

I rattle off the amenities, counting them on my fingers. "Let's see. I've got a full-time concierge, unlimited chocolate pudding, and laundry service. Oh, and Barb talked Dr. Hamid into letting me keep all my meds and treatments in my room this time! Check it out!"

I turn the webcam to the pile of medical equipment and then to the medicine cart next to me, which I've already perfectly organized into alphabetical *and* chronological order by the scheduled dosage time I plugged into the app I made. It's *finally* ready for a test run!

That was number 14 on today's to-do list, and I'm pretty proud of how it turned out.

My computer dings as comments begin rolling in. I see one mentioning Barb's name with some heart emojis. She's a crowd favorite just as much as she's my favorite. Ever since I first came to the hospital more than ten years ago, she's been the respiratory therapist here, slipping candy to me and the other CFers, like my partner in crime Poe. She holds our hand through even the most bone-crushing grips of pain like it's nothing.

I've been making YouTube videos for about half that time to raise awareness about cystic fibrosis. Through the years more people than I could have ever imagined began following my surgeries and my treatments and my visits to Saint Grace's, sticking with me through my awkward braces phase and everything.

"My lung function is down to thirty-five percent," I say as I turn the camera back to me. "Dr. Hamid says I'm steadily climbing to the top of the transplant list now, so I'll be here for a month, taking antibiotics, sticking to my regimen. . . ." My eyes travel to the drawing behind me, the healthy lungs looming over my head, just out of reach.

I shake my head and smile, leaning over to grab a bottle from the medicine cart. "That means taking my medications on time, wearing my AffloVest to break up that mucus, and"—I hold up the bottle—"a whole lot of this liquid nutrition through my G-tube every night. If any ladies out there are wishing they could eat five thousand calories a day and still have a Cabo-ready beach body, I'm up for a trade."

My computer dings away, messages pouring in one after another. Reading a few, I let the positivity push away all the negativity I felt going into this.

Hang in there, Stella! We love you.

Marry me!

"New lungs can come in *at any moment*, so I've got to be ready!" I say the words like I believe them wholeheartedly. Though after all these years I've learned to not get my hopes up too much.

DING! Another message.

I've got CF and you remind me to always stay positive. XOXO.

My heart warms, and I give a final big smile for the camera, for that person fighting the same fight that I am. This time it's genuine. "All right, guys, thanks for watching! Gotta double-check my afternoon and evening meds now. You know how anal I am. I hope everyone has a great week. Bye!"

I end the live video and exhale slowly, closing the browser to see the smiling, winter-formal-ready faces on my desktop background. Me, Camila, and Mya, arm in arm, all in the same deep-red lipstick we'd picked out together at Sephora. Camila had wanted a bright pink, but Mya had convinced us that red was the color we NEEDED in our life. I'm still not convinced that was true.

Lying back, I pick up the worn panda resting on my pillows and wrap my arms tightly around him. Patches, my sister, Abby, named him. And what a fitting name that became.

The years of coming in and out of the hospital with me have certainly taken their toll on him. Multicolored patches are sewn over spots where he ripped open, his stuffing pouring out when I squeezed too hard during the most painful of my treatments.

There's a knock on my door, and it flies open not even a second later as Barb busts in holding an armful of pudding cups for me to take my medication with. "I'm back! Delivery!"

When it comes to Barb, not much has changed in the past six months, or the past ten years for that matter; she's still the best. The same short, curly hair. The same colorful scrubs. The same smile that lights up the entire room.

But then an extremely pregnant Julie trails behind her, carrying an IV drip.

Now *that's* a big change from six months ago.

I swallow my surprise and grin at Barb as she places the pudding at the edge of my bed for me to sort onto my medicine cart, then pulls out a list to double-check that the cart has everything I need on it.

"What would I do without you?" I ask.

She winks. "You'd die."

Julie hangs the IV bag of antibiotics next to me, her belly brushing up against my arm. Why didn't she tell me she's pregnant? I go rigid, smiling thinly, as I eye her baby bump and try to subtly move away from it. "A lot's changed in the past six months!"

She rubs her belly, blue eyes shining brightly as she gives me a big smile. "You want to feel her kick?"

"No," I say, a little too quickly. I feel bad when she looks slightly taken aback at my bluntness, her blond eyebrows arching up in surprise. But I don't want any of my bad juju near that perfect, healthy baby.

Luckily, her eyes travel to my desktop background. "Are those your winter formal pics? I saw a bunch on Insta!" she says, excited. "How was it?"

"Super fun!" I say with a ton of enthusiasm as the awkwardness melts away. I open a folder on my desktop filled with pictures. "Crushed it on the dance floor for a solid three songs. Got to ride in a limo. The food didn't suck. Plus, I made it to ten thirty before I got tired, which was way better than expected! Who needs a curfew when your body does it for you, right?"

I show her and Barb some pictures we all took at Mya's house before the dance while she hooks me up to the IV drip and tests my blood pressure and O_2 reading. I remember I used to be afraid of needles, but with every blood draw and IV drip, that fear slowly drifted away. Now I don't even flinch. It makes me feel strong every time I get poked or prodded. Like I can overcome anything.

"All righty," Barb says when they get all my vitals and finish oohing and aahing over my sparkly, silver A-line gown and my white rose corsage. Camila, Mya, and I decided to swap corsages when we went stag to the formal. I didn't want to take a date, not that anybody asked me anyway. It was super possible that I would need to bail the day of, or wouldn't feel well halfway through the dance, which wouldn't have been fair to whomever I could've gone with. The two of them didn't want me to feel left out, so instead of getting dates of their own, they decided we'd all go together. Because of the Mason developments, though, that doesn't seem super likely for prom.

Barb nods to the filled medicine cart, resting a hand on her hip. "I'll still monitor you, but you're pretty much good to go." She holds up a pill bottle. "Remember, you *have* to take this one with food," she says, putting it carefully back and holding up another one. "And make sure you don't—"

"I got it, Barb," I say. She's just being her usual motherly self, but she holds up her hands in surrender. Deep down she knows that I'll be absolutely fine.

I wave good-bye as they both head toward the door, using the remote next to my bed to sit it up a little more.

"By the way," Barb says slowly as Julie ducks out of the room. Her eyes narrow at me and she gives me a gentle warning look. "I want you to finish your IV drip first, but Poe's just checked in to room 310."

"What? Really?" I say, my eyes widening as I move to launch myself out of bed to find him. I can't believe he didn't tell me he'd be here!

Barb steps forward, grabbing my shoulders and pushing

me gently back down onto the bed before I can fully stand. "What part of 'I want you to finish your IV drip first' did you not get?"

I smile sheepishly at her, but how could she blame me? Poe was the first friend I made when I came to the hospital. He's the only one who really gets it. We've fought CF together for a freaking decade. Well, together from a safe distance, anyway.

We can't get too close to each other. For cystic fibrosis patients, cross-infection from certain bacteria strains is a huge risk. One touch between two CFers can literally kill the both of them.

Her serious frown gives way to a gentle smile. "Settle in. Relax. Take a chill pill." She eyes the medicine cart, jokingly. "Not literally."

I nod, a real laugh spilling out, as a fresh wave of relief fills me at the news of Poe being here too.

"I'll stop by later to help you with your AffloVest," Barb says over her shoulder as she leaves. Grabbing my phone, I settle for a quick text message instead of a mad dash down the hall to room 310.

You're here? Me too. Tune-up.

Not even a second goes by and my screen lights up with his reply: Bronchitis. Just happened. I'll live. Come by and wave at me later. Gonna crash now.

I lean back on the bed, exhaling long and slow.

Truth is, I'm nervous about this visit.

My lung function fell to 35 percent so quickly. And now, even more than the fever and the sore throat, being here in the hospital for the next month doing treatment after treatment to stem the tide while my friends are far away is freaking me out. A lot. Thirty-five percent is a number that keeps my mom up at night. She doesn't say it, but her computer does. Search after search about lung transplants and lung-function percentages, new combinations and phrasing but always the same idea. How to get me more time. It makes me more afraid than I've ever been before. But not for me. When you have CF, you sort of get used to the idea of dying young. No, I'm terrified for my parents. And what will become of them if the worst does happen, now that they don't have each other.

But with Poe here, someone who *understands*, I can get through it. Once I'm actually allowed to see him.

The rest of the afternoon goes by slowly.

I work on my app, double-checking that I worked out the programming error that kept coming up when I tried to run it on my phone. I put some Fucidin on the sore skin around my G-tube in an attempt to make it less fire-engine red and more of a summer-sunset pink. I check and double-check my "At Bedtime" pile of bottles and pills. I reply to my parents' every-hour-on-the-hour texts. I gaze out the window as the afternoon fades and see a couple about my age, laughing and kissing as they walk into the hospital. It's not every day you see a happy couple coming into a hospital. Watching them holding hands and exchanging longing glances, I wonder what it would be like to have somebody look at me like that. People are always looking at my cannula, my scars, my G-tube, not at *me.*

It doesn't make guys want to line up by my locker.

I "dated" Tyler Paul my freshman year of high school, but that lasted all of a month, until I came down with an infection and needed to go to the hospital for a few weeks. Even just a few days in, his texts started to get further and further apart, and I decided to break up with him. Besides, it was nothing like that couple out in the courtyard. Tyler's palms were sweaty when we held hands, and he wore so much Axe body spray, I would go into coughing fits every time we hugged.

This thought process is not exactly a helpful distraction, so I even give number 22, "Contemplate the afterlife," on my to-do list a try, and read some of *Life, Death, and Immortality: The Journey of the Soul.*

But, pretty soon, I opt to just lie on my bed, looking up at the ceiling and listening to the wheezing sound of my breathing. I can hear the air struggling to get past the mucus that takes up space in my lungs. Rolling over, I crack open a vial of Flovent to give my lungs a helping hand. I pour the liquid into a nebulizer by my bed, the small machine humming to life as vapors pour from the mouthpiece.

I sit, staring at the drawing of the lungs while I breathe in and out.

And in and out.

And in and . . . out.

I hope when my parents come to visit over the next few days, my breathing is a little less labored. I told them both that the other one was taking me to the hospital this morning, but I actually just took an Uber here from the corner a street over from my mom's new place. I don't want either of them to have to face seeing me here again, at least until I'm looking better.

My mom was already giving me troubled looks when I needed to put my portable oxygen on just to pack.

There's a knock on my door, and I look over from the wall I'm staring at, hoping it's Poe stopping by to wave at me. I pull the mouthpiece off as Barb pops her head in. She drops a surgical face mask and latex gloves onto a table next to my door.

"New one upstairs. Meet me in fifteen?"

My heart leaps.

I nod, and she gives me a big smile before ducking out of the room. I grab the mouthpiece and take one more quick hit of the Flovent, letting the vapor fill my lungs the best I can before I'm up and moving. Shutting the nebulizer off, I pick up my portable oxygen concentrator from where it's been charging next to my bed, press the circular button in the center to turn it on, and pull the strap over my shoulder. After I put the cannula in, I head over to the door, pulling on the blue latex gloves and wrapping the strings of the face mask around my ears.

Sliding into my white Converse, I push my door open then squeeze out into the whitewashed corridor, deciding to go the long way so I can walk past Poe's room.

I pass the nurses' station in the center of the floor, waving hello to a young nurse's assistant named Sarah, who is smiling over the top of the new, sleek metal cubicle.

They replaced that before my last visit six months ago. It's the same height, but it used to be made of this worn wood that had probably been around since the hospital was founded sixty-some years ago. I remember when I was small enough to sneak past to whatever room Poe was in, my head still a good few inches from clearing the desk.

Now it comes up to my elbow.

Heading down the hallway, I grin as I see a small Colombian flag taped on the outside of a half-open door, an overturned skateboard keeping it propped slightly open.

I peer inside to see Poe fast asleep on his bed, curled into a surprisingly tiny ball underneath his plaid comforter, a suave Gordon Ramsay poster, positioned directly over his bed, keeping watch over him.

I draw a heart on the dry-erase board he's stuck to the outside of his door to let him know I've been there, before moving off down the hallway toward the wooden double doors that will take me to the main part of the hospital, up an elevator, down C Wing, across the bridge into Building 2, and straight to the Neonatal Intensive Care Unit.

One of the perks of coming here for more than a decade is that I know the hospital just as well as I knew the house I grew up in. Every winding corridor, or hidden staircase, or secret shortcut, explored over and over again.

But before I can open the double doors, a room door swings open next to me, and I turn my head in surprise to see the profile of a tall, thin boy I've never seen before. He's standing in the doorway of room 315, holding a sketchbook in one hand and a charcoal pencil in the other, a white hospital bracelet like mine wrapped around his wrist.

I stop dead.

His tousled, dark-chocolate-brown hair is perfectly unruly, like he just popped out of a *Teen Vogue* and landed smack in the middle of Saint Grace's Hospital. His eyes are a deep blue, the corners crinkling as he talks.

But it's his smile that catches my eye more than anything else. It's lopsided, and charming, and it has a magnetic warmth to it.

He's so cute, my lung function feels like it dropped another 10 percent.

It's a good thing this mask is covering half my face, because I did not plan for cute guys on my floor this hospital stay.

"I've clocked their schedules," he says as he puts the pencil casually behind his ear. I shift slightly to the left and see that he's grinning at the couple I saw coming into the hospital earlier. "So, unless you plant your ass on the call button, no one's going to bother you for at *least* an hour. And don't forget. I gotta sleep in that bed, dude."

"Way ahead of you." I watch as the girl unzips the duffel bag she's holding to show him blankets.

Wait. What?

Cute guy whistles. "Look at that. A regular Girl Scout."

"We're not animals, man," her boyfriend says to him, giving him a big, dude-to-dude smile.

Oh my god. Gross. He's letting his friends do it in his room, like it's a motel.

I grimace and resume walking down the hallway to the exit doors, putting as much space as possible between me and whatever scheme is going on in there.

So much for cute.

CHAPTER 2

WILL

"All right, I'll see you guys later," I say, winking at Jason and closing the door to my room to give them some privacy. I come face-to-face with the empty sockets of the skull drawing on my door, an O_2 mask slung over its mouth, with the words "Abandon all hope, ye who enter here" written under it.

That should be the slogan for this hospital. Or any of the other fifty I've been in for the past eight months of my life.

I squint down the hallway to see the door swinging shut behind the girl I saw moving into a room down the hall earlier today, her scuffed white Converse disappearing onto the other side. She'd been by herself, lugging a duffel bag big enough for about three fully grown adults, but she actually looked kind of hot.

And, let's be honest here. It's not every day you see a remotely attractive girl hanging around a hospital, no more than five doors down from yours.

Looking down at my sketchbook, I shrug, rolling it up and stuffing it into my back pocket before heading down the hallway after her. It's not like I have anything better to do, and I'm certainly not trying to stick around here for the next hour.

Pushing through the doors, I see her making her way across the gray tile floor, waving and chatting to just about everyone as she goes, like she's putting on her own personal Thanksgiving Day Parade. She steps onto the large glass elevator, overlooking the east lobby, just past a large, decked-out Christmas tree they must've put up early this morning, long before the Thanksgiving leftovers were even eaten.

Heaven forbid they leave up the giant turkey display for even a minute longer.

I watch as her hands reach up to fix her face mask while she leans over to press a button, the doors slowly closing.

I start climbing the open stairs by the elevator, trying not to run into anyone as I watch it chug steadily to the fifth floor. Of course. I run up the stairs as fast as my lungs will carry me, managing to get to the fifth floor with enough time to go into a serious coughing fit *and* recover before she exits the elevator and disappears around a corner. I rub my chest, clearing my throat and following her down a couple of hallways and onto the wide, glass-encased bridge leading to the next building.

Even though she just got here this morning, she clearly knows where she's going. Judging from her pace and the fact she apparently knows every single person in the building, I wouldn't be surprised if she were actually the mayor of this place. I've been here two weeks, and it took me until yesterday to figure out how to sneak safely from my room to the cafeteria over in Building 2, and I am by no means directionally challenged. I've been in so many hospitals over the years, figuring out how to get around them is what counts as a hobby to me now.

She stops short under a set of double doors reading EAST ENTRANCE: NEONATAL INTENSIVE CARE UNIT and peeks inside before she pushes them open.

The NICU.

Odd.

Having kids when you have CF falls into the super difficult category. I've heard of girls with CF bumming *hard* over it, but going to stare at the babies she might never have is a whole other level.

That's just fucking depressing.

There are a lot of things that piss me off about CF, but that's not one of them. Pretty much all guys with CF are infertile, which at least means I don't have to worry about getting anyone pregnant and starting my own shit show of a family.

Bet Jason wishes he had that going for him right now.

Looking both ways, I close the gap between me and the doors, peering inside the narrow window to see her standing in front of the viewing pane, her eyes focused on a small baby inside an incubator on the other side. Its fragile arms and legs are hooked up to machines ten times its size.

Pushing open the door and sliding inside the dimly lit hallway, I smile as I watch Converse girl for a second. I can't help but stare at her reflection, everything beyond the glass blurring as I look at her. She's prettier close up, with her long eyelashes and her full eyebrows. She even makes a face mask look good. I watch as she brushes her wavy, sandy-brown hair out of her eyes, staring at the baby through the glass with a determined focus.

I clear my throat, getting her attention. "And here I thought this was gonna be another lame hospital filled with lame sickies. But then you show up. Lucky me."

Her eyes meet mine in the reflection of the glass, surprise filling them at first, and then almost immediately changing to something resembling disgust. She looks away, back at the baby, staying silent.

Well, that's always a promising sign. Nothing like actual repulsion to start off on the right foot.

"I saw you moving into your room. Gonna be here awhile?"

She doesn't say anything. If it wasn't for the grimace, I'd think she didn't even hear me.

"Oh, I get it. I'm so good looking you can't even string a sentence together."

That annoys her enough to get a response.

"Shouldn't you be procuring rooms for your 'guests'?" she snaps, turning to face me as she angrily pulls her face mask off.

She takes me off guard for a second, and I laugh, surprised by how up-front she is.

That *really* pisses her off.

"You rent by the hour, or what?" she asks, her dark eyes narrowing.

"Ha! It *was* you lurking in the hall."

"I don't *lurk*," she fires back. "*You* followed *me* here."

It's a valid point. But she definitely lurked first. I pretend to be taken aback and hold up my hands in mock defeat. "With the intent of introducing myself, but with that attitude—"

"Let me guess," she says, cutting me off. "You consider yourself a rebel. Ignoring the rules because it somehow makes you feel in control. Am I right?"

"You're not wrong," I shoot back before leaning against the wall casually.

"You think it's cute?"

I grin at her. "I mean, you must think it's pretty adorable. You stood in the hallway an awfully long time staring."

She rolls her eyes, clearly not entertained by me. "You letting your friends borrow your room for sex isn't cute."

Ah, so she's a real goody two shoes.

"Sex? Oh, heavens no. They told me they would be holding a slightly rowdy book club meeting in there for the better part of an hour."

She glares at me, definitely not amused by my sarcasm.

"Ah. So that's what this is about," I say, crossing my arms over my chest. "You have something against sex."

"Of course not! I've had sex," she says, her eyes widening as the words tumble out of her mouth. "It's *fine*—"

That is the biggest lie I've heard all year, and I'm practically surrounded by people who sugarcoat the fact that I'm dying.

I laugh. "'Fine' isn't exactly a ringing endorsement, but I'll take common ground where I can get it."

Her thick eyebrows form a frown. "We have *nothing* in common."

I wink, having way too much fun pissing her off. "Cold. I like it."

The door bangs open and Barb busts through, making both of us jump in surprise at the sudden noise. "Will Newman! What are you doing up here? You're not supposed to leave the third floor after that stunt you pulled last week!"

I look back at the girl. "There you go. A name to go with your little psych profile. And you are?"

She glowers at me, quickly pulling her face mask back over her mouth before Barb notices. "Ignoring you."

Good one. Ms. Goody Two Shoes has some spunk.

"And clearly the teacher's pet, too."

"Six feet at all times! You both know the rules!" I realize I'm too close and take a step back as Barb reaches us, coming into the space and the tension between us. She turns to look at me, her eyes narrowing. "What do you think you're doing up here?"

"Uh," I say, pointing at the viewing window. "Looking at babies?"

She's clearly not amused. "Get back to your room. Where is your face mask?" I reach up to touch my maskless face. "Stella, thank you for keeping your mask on."

"She didn't five seconds ago," I mutter. Stella glares at me over Barb's head, and I give her back a big smile.

Stella.

Her name is Stella.

I can see Barb's about to really ream me out, so I decide to make my exit. I've had more than enough lecturing for the moment.

"Lighten up, Stella," I say, sauntering to the door. "It's just life. It'll be over before we know it."

I head out through the doors, across the bridge, and down C Wing. Instead of going back the long way, I hop on a much shakier, nonglass elevator, which I discovered two days ago. It spits me out right by the nurses' station on my floor, where Julie is reading over some paperwork.

"Hey, Julie," I say, leaning on the counter and picking up a pencil.

She glances up at me, giving me a quick look, before her eyes swing back down to the papers in her hands. "Just what were you up to?"

"Eh, roaming the hospital. Pissing off Barb," I say, shrugging and twirling the pencil around and around in my fingertips. "She's *such* a hard-ass."

"Will, she's not a hard-ass, she's just, you know . . ."

I give her a look. "A hard-ass."

She leans against the nurses' station, putting a hand on her super-pregnant belly. "Firm. The rules matter. Especially to Barb. She doesn't take chances."

I glance over to see the doors at the end of the hallway swing wide open again as Barb and the goody-goody herself step out.

Barb's eyes narrow at me and I shrug innocently. "What? I'm talking to Julie."

She huffs, and the two of them walk off down the hallway toward Stella's room. Stella fixes her face mask, looking back at me, her eyes meeting mine for a fraction of a second.

I sigh, watching her go.

"She hates me."

"Which one?" Julie asks, following my gaze down the hallway.

The door to Stella's room closes behind the both of them, and I look back at Julie.

She gives me a look that I've seen about a million times since I got here. Her blue eyes fill with a mix between *Are you crazy?* and something very close to care.

Mostly *Are you crazy?* though.

"Don't even *think* about it, Will."

I glance down at the file sitting in front of her, the name jumping out at me from the upper left-hand corner.

Stella Grant.

"Okay," I say like it's no big deal. "Night."

I stroll back to 315, coughing when I get there, the mucus thick in my lungs and throat, my chest aching from my excursion. If I had known I was going to be running a half marathon all around the hospital, I might've bothered to bring my portable oxygen.

Eh, who am I kidding?

I check my watch to make sure it's been an hour before pushing open the door. I flick on the light, noticing a folded note from Hope and Jason on the bleach-white standard-issue hospital sheets.

How romantic of them.

I try not to be disappointed they're already gone. My mom pulled me out of school and switched me to homeschooling with a side of international hospital tourism when I got diagnosed with B. cepacia eight months ago. As if my life span wasn't already going to be ridiculously short, B. cepacia will cut off another huge chunk of it by making my shitty lung function deplete even faster than it already has. And they don't give you new lungs when you have an antibiotic-resistant bacteria running rampant inside of you.

But "incurable" is only a suggestion to my mother, and

she's determined to find the needle-in-a-haystack treatment. Even if it means cutting me off from everyone.

At least this hospital is half an hour away from Hope and Jason, so they can come visit me on a regular basis and fill me in on everything I'm missing at school. Since I got B. cepacia, I feel like they're the only ones in my life who don't treat me like a lab rat. They've always been that way; maybe that's why they're so perfect for each other.

I unfold the note to see a heart and, in Hope's neat cursive, "See you soon! Two weeks till your Big 18! Hope and Jason." And that makes me smile.

"Big 18." Two more weeks until I'm in charge. I'll be off this latest clinical drug trial and out of this hospital and can do something with my life, instead of letting my mom waste it.

No more hospitals. No more being stuck inside white-washed buildings all over the world as doctors try drug after drug, treatment after treatment, none of them working.

If I'm going to die, I'd like to actually *live* first.

And *then* I'll die.

I squint at the heart, thinking about that fateful last day. Somewhere poetic. A beach, maybe. Or a rowboat somewhere in Mississippi. Just no walls. I could sketch the landscape, draw a final cartoon of me giving the middle finger to the universe, then bite the big one.

I toss the note back onto the bed, eyeing the sheets before

giving them a quick whiff to be safe. Starch and bleach. Just the regular hospital eau de cologne. Good.

I slide into the squeaky leather hospital recliner by the window and push aside a heap of colored pencils and sketchbooks, grabbing my laptop from under a bunch of photocopied 1940s political cartoons I was looking at earlier for reference. I open my browser and type *Stella Grant* into Google, not expecting much. She seems like the type to have only the most private of Facebook pages. Or a lame Twitter account where she retweets memes about the importance of hand washing.

The first result, though, is a YouTube page called *Stella Grant's Not-So-Secret CF Diary,* filled with at least a hundred videos dating back six years or so. I squint, because the page name looks weirdly familiar. Oh my god, this is that lame channel my mom sent me a link to a few months ago in an attempt to rally me into taking my treatments seriously.

Maybe if I'd known she looked like that . . .

I scroll down to the first entry, clicking on a video with a thumbnail of a young Stella wearing a mouthful of metal and a high ponytail. I try not to laugh. I wonder what her teeth look like now, considering I've never seen her smile.

Probably pretty nice. She seems like the type who would actually wear her retainer at night instead of letting it collect dust on some bathroom shelf.

I don't think mine even made it home from the orthodontist.

I hit the volume button and her voice comes pouring out of my speakers.

"Like all CFers, I was born terminal. Our bodies make too much mucus, and that mucus likes to get into our lungs and cause infections, making our lung function de-teri-orate." The young girl stumbles over the big word before flashing the camera a big smile. "Right now, I'm at fifty percent lung function."

There's a crappy cut, and she turns around on a set of stairs that I recognize from the main entrance of the hospital. No wonder she knows her way around here so well. She's been coming here forever.

I smile back at the little girl even though that cut was the cheesiest thing I've ever seen. She sits down on the steps, taking a deep breath. "Dr. Hamid says, at this rate, I'm gonna need a transplant by the time I'm in high school. A transplant's not a cure, but it will give me more time! I'd love a few more years if I'm lucky enough to get one!"

Tell me about it, Stella.

At least she's got a shot.

CHAPTER 3

STELLA

I pull on the blue AffloVest, snapping it into place around my torso with Barb's help. It looks an awful lot like a life vest, except for the remote coming out of it. For the quickest moment I let it be a life vest, and I stare out the window, picturing myself in Cabo on a boat with Mya and Camila, the afternoon sun glowing on the horizon.

The seagulls chirping, the sandy beach in the distance, the shirtless surfers—and then, despite myself, I think of Will. I blink, Cabo fading away as the barren trees outside my window swing into view.

"So, Will. He's a CFer, then?" I ask, though that's obvious. Barb helps me clip the last strap into place. I pull at the shoulder of the vest so it doesn't rub into my bony collarbone.

"A CFer and then some. B. cepacia. He's part of the new drug trial for Cevaflomalin." She reaches over, flicking the machine on and giving me a look.

My eyes widen and I look over at my giant tub of hand sanitizer. I was that close to him and he has *B. cepacia*? It's pretty much a death sentence for people with CF. He'll be lucky to make it a few more years.

And that's if he's as dedicated to his regimen as I am.

The vest begins vibrating. Hard. I can feel the mucus in my lungs starting to slowly loosen.

"You contract that and you can kiss the possibility of new lungs good-bye," she adds, eyeing me. "Stay away."

I nod. Oh, I fully intend to do just that. I need that extra time. Besides, he was way too full of himself to be my type. "The trial," I start to say, looking over at Barb and holding up my hand to pause the conversation as I cough up a wad of mucus.

She nods in approval and hands me a standard-issue pale-pink bedpan. I spit into it and wipe my mouth before talking.

"What are his odds?"

Barb exhales, shaking her head before meeting my gaze. "Nobody knows. The drug's too new."

Her look says it all, though. We fall silent except for the chugging of the machine, the vest vibrating away.

"You're set. Need anything before I hit the road?"

I grin at her, giving her a pleading look. "A milk shake?"

She rolls her eyes, putting her hands on her hips. "What, am I room service now?"

"Gotta take advantage of the perks, Barb!" I say, which makes her laugh.

She leaves, and I sit back, the AffloVest making my whole body shake as it works. My mind wanders, and I picture Will's reflection in the glass of the NICU, standing just behind me with a daring smile on his face.

B. cepacia. That's rough.

But walking around the hospital without a mask on? It's no wonder he got it in the first place, pulling stunts like that. I've seen his type in the hospital more times than I can count. The careless, *Braveheart* type, rebelling in a desperate attempt to defy their diagnosis before it all comes to an end. It's not even original.

"All right," Barb says, bringing me not one but *two* milk shakes, like the queen she is. "This should hold you over for a bit."

She puts them on the table next to me, and I smile up at her familiar dark-brown eyes. "Thanks, Barb."

She nods, touching my head gently before heading out the door. "Night, baby. See you tomorrow."

I sit, staring out the window and coughing up more and more mucus as the vest does its job to clear my airways. My eyes travel to the drawing of the lungs and the picture hanging next to it. My chest starts to hurt in a way that has nothing to do with the treatment as I think of my real bed. My parents. Abby. I pick up my phone to see a text from my dad. It's a picture of his old acoustic guitar, leaning against a worn nightstand in his new apartment. He spent the whole day setting it up after I insisted he do that instead of take me to the hospital. He pretended not to be relieved, just like I pretended Mom was taking me so he wouldn't feel guilty.

It's been a lot of pretending since the most ridiculous divorce of all time.

It's been six months and they still can't even look at each other.

For some reason it makes me want to hear his voice so badly. I tap on his contact info and almost press the green call button on my phone, but decide not to at the last second. I never call the first day, and all the coughing that the AffloVest makes me do would make him nervous. He's still texting me every hour to check in.

I don't want to worry my parents. I *can't*.

Better to just wait until morning.

My eyes shoot open the next morning and I look for what woke me, seeing my phone vibrating noisily on the floor, having free-fallen off the table. I squint at the drained milkshake glasses and mound of empty chocolate pudding cups taking up practically the entire space. No wonder the phone fell off.

If we're 60 percent water, I'm closing in on the remaining 40 percent being pudding.

I groan, reaching over the bed to grab my phone, my G-tube burning with the stretch. I gently touch my side, lifting my shirt to unhook the tube, surprised that the skin around it is even redder and more inflamed than it was before.

That's not good. Irritations usually go away with a little bit of Fucidin, but my application yesterday didn't seem to make a difference.

I put a bigger glob of the ointment on it, hoping that will clear it up, and add a note to my to-do list to monitor it, before scrolling through my notifications. I have a couple of Snaps waiting from Mya and Camila, looking sleepy but happy as they boarded the plane this morning. Both of my parents texted me, checking in to see how I slept, if I'm settled in, and saying to give them a call when I get up.

I'm about to answer the both of them when my phone vibrates, and I swipe right to see a text from Poe: You up?

I shoot back a quick message seeing if he wants to have our usual breakfast date in twenty, before putting the phone down and swinging my legs over my bed to grab my laptop.

Less than a second later my phone buzzes with his reply: Yees!

I grin, hitting the nurse-call button by my bed. Julie's friendly voice crackles through the speaker. "Morning, Stella! You good?"

"Yep. Can I get breakfast now?" I ask, turning my laptop on.

"You got it!"

The time on my laptop reads 9:00 a.m., and I pull the med cart closer, looking at the color-coded clumps I laid out yesterday. I smile to myself, realizing that this time tomorrow, after I get the beta version of my app fully up and running, I'll be getting a notification on my phone telling me to take my morning pills and the exact dosages of each that I need.

Almost a *year* of hard work finally coming together. An app for all chronic illnesses, complete with med charts, schedules, and dosage information.

I take my pills and open Skype, scanning the contact list to see if either of my parents is on. There's a tiny green dot next to my dad's name, and I press the call button, waiting as it rings noisily.

His face appears on the screen as he puts his thick-rim glasses over his tired eyes. I notice that he's still in his pajamas, his graying hair jutting out in every direction, a lumpy pillow propped up behind him. Dad was always an early riser. Out of bed before seven thirty every morning, even on the weekends.

The worry starts to slowly wrap itself tighter around my insides.

"You need a shave," I say, taking in the unusual stubble covering his chin. He's always been clean shaven, except for a beard phase he went through one winter during elementary school.

He chuckles, rubbing his scruffy chin. "You need new lungs. Mic drop!"

I roll my eyes as he laughs at his own joke. "How was the gig?"

He shrugs. "Eh, you know."

"I'm glad you're performing again!" I say cheerily, trying my best to look positive for him.

"Sore throat doing okay?" he asks, giving me a worried look.

I nod, swallowing to confirm that the rawness in my throat has started to subside. "Already a million times better!" Relief fills his eyes, and I change the subject quickly before he can ask any more treatment-related questions. "How's your new apartment?"

He gives me an over-the-top smile. "It's great! It's got a bed *and* a bathroom!" His smile fades slightly, and he shrugs. "And not much else. I'm sure your mom's place is nicer. She could always make anywhere feel like home."

"Maybe if you just call her—"

He shakes his head at me and cuts me off. "Moving on. Seriously, it's fine, hun. The place is great, and I've got you and my guitar! What else do I need?"

My stomach clenches, but there's a knock on my door and Julie comes in, holding a dark-green tray with a pile of food.

My dad sees her and brightens up. "Julie! How've you been?"

Julie puts down the tray and presents her belly to him. For someone who insisted for the past five years that she was never having children, she seems ridiculously eager to be having children.

"Very busy, I see," my dad says, smiling wide.

"Talk to you later, Dad," I say, moving my cursor over to the end-call button. "Love you."

He gives me a salute before the chat ends. The smell of eggs and bacon wafts off the plate, a giant chocolate milk shake sitting on the tray next to it.

"Need anything else, Stell? Some company?"

I glance at her baby bump, shaking my head as a surprising swell of contempt fills my chest. I love Julie, but I'm really not in the mood for talking about her new little family when mine's falling apart. "Poe's about to call me."

Right on time, my laptop pings and Poe's picture pops up, the green phone symbol appearing on my screen. Julie rubs her stomach, giving me a strange look before flashing me a tight-lipped, confused smile. "Okay. You two have fun!"

I press accept and Poe's face slowly comes into view, his thick black eyebrows hanging over familiar warm brown eyes. He's gotten a haircut since the last time I saw him. Shorter. Cleaner. He gives me a big ear-to-ear smile, and I attempt to grin back, but it ends up looking more like a grimace.

I can't get the image of my dad out of my head. So sad and alone, in bed, but the lines of his face still deep and filled with exhaustion.

And I can't even go check on him.

“Hey, *mami*! You are looking WORN,” he says, putting his milk shake down and squinting at me. “You go on one of your chocolate pudding benders again?”

I know this is where I’m supposed to laugh, but I seem to have used up my pretending quota for the day, and it’s not even nine thirty yet.

Poe frowns. “Uh-oh. What’s wrong? Is it Cabo? You know sunburn is nothing to play with anyway.”

I wave that away and instead hold up my tray like a game-show model to show Poe my lumberjack breakfast. Eggs, bacon, potatoes, and a milk shake! The usual for our breakfast dates.

Poe gives me a challenging look, like I’m not getting away with that subject change, but he can’t resist holding up his plate to show me the identical meal—except his eggs are beautifully embellished with chives, parsley, and . . . Wait.

Freaking truffles!

“Poe! Where the hell did you get truffles?”

He raises his eyebrows, smirking. “You gotta bring ’em with, *mija*!” he says as he moves the webcam to show me a med cart that he’s converted into a perfectly organized spice rack. It’s filled with jars and specialty items instead of pill bottles, sitting under his shrine to his favorite skateboarder, Paul Rodriguez, and the entire Colombian national soccer team. Classic Poe. Food, skateboarding, and *fútbol* are by FAR his three favorite things.

He has enough jerseys pinned up on his wall to fully clothe every CFer on this floor for a poor-playing, no-cardiovascular-strength B-team.

The camera swings back to him, and I see Gordon Ramsay's chest peering out from behind him. "But first—our appetizers!" He holds up a handful of Creon tablets, which will help our bodies digest the food we're about to eat.

"Best part of every meal!" I say sarcastically as I scoop my red-and-white tablets out of a small plastic cup next to my tray.

"So," Poe says after he's swallowed his last one. "Since you won't spill, let's talk about me. I'm single! Ready to—"

"You broke up with Michael?" I ask, exasperated. "Poe!"

Poe takes a long sip of his milk shake. "Maybe he broke up with me."

"Did he?"

"Yes! Well, it was mutual," he says, before sighing and shaking his head. "Whatever. I broke up with him."

I frown. They were perfect for each other. Michael liked skateboarding and had a super-popular food blog that Poe had followed religiously for three years before they met. He was different from the other people Poe had dated. Older, somehow, even though he had just turned eighteen. Most importantly, Poe was different with him. "You really liked him, Poe. I thought he might be the one."

But I should know better; Poe could write a book on

commitment issues. Still, that never stopped him on the quest for another great romance. Before Michael it was Tim, the week after this it could be David. And, to be honest, I envy him a bit, with his wild romances.

I've never been in love before. Tyler Paul for sure didn't count. But even if I had the chance, dating is a risk that I can't afford right now. I have to stay focused. Keep myself alive. Get my transplant. Reduce parental misery. It's pretty much a full-time job. And definitely not a sexy one.

"Well, he's not," Poe says, acting like it's no big deal. "Screw him anyway, right?"

"Hey, at least you got to do that," I say, shrugging as I pick at my eggs. I can see Will's knowing smirk from yesterday when I told him I'd had sex before. Asshole.

Poe laughs midsip of his milk shake, but he sputters and begins to choke. His vital monitors start beeping on the other side of the laptop as he struggles for breath.

Oh my god. No, no, no. I jump up. "Poe!"

I push aside the laptop and run into the hallway as an alarm sounds at the nurses' station, fear in every pore of my body. Somewhere a voice shouts out, "Room 310! Blood oxygen level is in free fall. He's desatting!"

Desatting. He can't breathe, he can't breathe. "He's choking! Poe's choking!" I shout out, tears filling my eyes as I fly down the hallway behind Julie, pulling on a face mask as I go. She bursts through the door ahead of me and goes to check the beeping monitor. I'm scared to look. I'm scared to see Poe suffering. I'm scared to see Poe . . .

Fine.

He's fine, sitting in his chair like nothing happened.

Relief floods through me and I break out in a cold sweat as he looks from me to Julie, a sheepish expression on his face as he holds up his fingertip sensor. "Sorry! It came unplugged. I didn't tape it back down after my shower."

I exhale slowly, realizing I've been holding my breath this whole time. Which is pretty hard to do when you have lungs that barely work.

Julie leans against the wall, looking just as shocked as I am. "Poe. Jeez. When your O_2 drops like that . . ." She shakes her head. "Just put it back on."

"I don't need it anymore, Jules," he says, looking up at her. "Let me take it off."

"Absolutely not. Your lung function sucks right now. We've gotta keep an eye on you, so you need to keep that damn thing on." She takes a deep breath, holding out a piece of tape so he can tape the sensor back on. "Please."

He sighs loudly but reattaches the fingertip sensor to the blood-oxygen sensor worn on his wrist.

I nod, finally catching my breath. "I agree, Poe. Keep it on."

He glances up at me as he tapes the sensor onto his middle finger, holding it up to me and grinning.

I roll my eyes at him, glancing down the hallway to the asshole's room: 315. The door is tightly closed despite the commotion, a light shining out from under it. He's not even going to poke his head out to make sure everybody's okay? This was practically a floor roll call, as everyone opened their door to double-check that everything was fine. I fidget and smooth my hair down, looking back over at Poe in time to see him raise his eyebrows at me.

"What, you trying to look good for someone?"

"Don't be ridiculous." I glare at him and Julie as they shoot curious looks in my direction. I point at his food. "You're about to waste some perfectly good truffles on a bunch of cold eggs," I say, before hurrying off down the hallway to finish our breakfast chat. The more space between room 315 and me the better.

CHAPTER 4

WILL

I rub my eyes sleepily, clicking on another video, my half-eaten tray of eggs and bacon sitting cold on the table next to me. I've been up all night watching her videos, one after the other. It's been a Stella Grant marathon, even with the lame CF content.

Scanning the sidebar, I click on the next one.

This one's from last year, the lighting ridiculously dark, except for the bright flash of her phone's camera. It looks like a fundraising event, held at a dimly lit bar. There's a huge banner dangling over a stage reading: SAVE THE PLANET—SUPPORT EARTH DAY.

The camera focuses on a man playing an acoustic guitar, sitting casually on a wooden stool, while a curly-brown-haired girl sings. I recognize them both from all the videos I've watched.

Stella's dad and her sister, Abby.

The view spins onto Stella, a big smile on her face, her teeth as white and even as I predicted. She's wearing makeup, and I cough in surprise at how different she looks. It's not the makeup, though. She's happier. Calmer. Not like she's been in person.

Even the nose cannula looks good on her when she smiles like that.

"Dad and Abby! Stealing the show! If I die before I'm twenty-one, at least I've been in a bar." She swings the camera to show an older woman with the same long brown hair sitting next to her in a bright-red booth. "Say hi, Mom!"

The woman waves, giving the camera a big grin.

A waitress passes by their table and Stella waves her down. "Ah, yes. I'll take a bourbon, please. Neat."

I snort as her mom's voice screams out a "No, she won't!"

"Ahh, nice try, Stella," I say, laughing as a bright light comes on, illuminating their faces.

The song in the background ends and Stella begins clapping manically, turning the camera to show her sister, Abby, smiling at her from the stage.

"So, my little sister, Stella, is here tonight," she says, pointing directly at Stella. "As if fighting for her own life isn't enough, she's going to save the planet, too! Come show 'em whatcha got, Stella!"

Stella's voice comes through my speakers, confused and shocked. "Uh, did you guys plan this?"

The camera swings back to her mom, who grins. Yep.

"Go on, baby. I'll film it!" her mom says, and everything swings out of focus as Stella hands over the phone.

Everyone in the room cheers as she pulls her portable oxygen concentrator onto the stage, her sister, Abby, helping her maneuver up the steps and into the spotlight. She adjusts her cannula nervously as her dad hands her a microphone, before she turns to the crowd and speaks. "This is a first for me. In front of a crowd, anyway. Don't laugh!"

So, naturally, everyone laughs, including Stella. Only, her laugh is filled with nerves.

She looks over at her sister warily. Abby says something to her that the microphone just barely picks up.

"Bushel and a peck."

What does *that* mean?

It works, though, and like magic the nervousness melts away from Stella's face.

Her dad starts to strum away at his guitar and I hum along before my brain even consciously registers what they're singing. Everyone in the audience is swaying along too, heads moving left and right, feet tapping with the beat.

"Now I've heard there was a secret chord . . ."

Wow. They both can *sing.*

Her sister is rocking this clear and strong and powerful voice, while Stella's is breathy and soft, smooth in all the right ways.

I hit pause as the camera closes in on Stella's face, all her features coming alive in the glow of the spotlight. Carefree, and smiling, and *happy*, up there onstage next to her sister and her dad. I wonder what made her so . . . uptight yesterday.

I run my fingers through my hair, taking in her long hair, the shadow of her collarbone, the way her brown eyes shine when she smiles. Her adrenaline gives her face a twinge of color, her cheeks a bright, exhilarated pink.

Not gonna lie. She's pretty.

Really pretty.

I look away and—wait a second. There's no way. I highlight the number with my cursor.

"A hundred thousand views? Are you kidding me?"

Who *is* this girl?

Not even an hour later, my first post-all-nighter nap was interrupted by a blaring alarm down the hall, and then my second attempt was foiled later by my mom and Dr. Hamid busting into my room for an evening visit. Bored, I stifle a yawn and stare out at the empty courtyard, the cold winds and the forecast of snow driving everyone inside.

Snow. At least that's something to look forward to.

I rest my head against the cool glass, eager for the world outside to be covered in a blanket of white. I haven't touched snow since the first time my mom shipped me off to a top-of-the-line treatment facility to be a guinea pig for an experimental drug to fight B. cepacia. It was in Sweden, and they'd been perfecting this thing for half a decade.

Clearly, it wasn't "perfected" enough, because I was out of there and back home in about two weeks flat.

At this point I don't remember much from that particular stay. The only thing I remember from most of my hospital trips is white. White hospital sheets, white walls, white lab coats, all running together. But I do remember the mountains and mountains of snow that fell while I was there, the same white, only beautiful, less sterile. Real. I'd been dreaming of going skiing in the Alps, lung function be damned. But the only snow I got to touch was on the roof of my mom's Mercedes rental.

"Will," my mother's voice says, sternly, cutting right through my daydream of fresh powder. "Are you listening?"

Is she kidding?

I turn my head to look at her and Dr. Hamid, and nod like a bobblehead even though I haven't heard a single word this entire time. They're going over my first test results since I started the trial a week or so ago, and as usual, nothing's changed.

"We need to be patient," Dr. Hamid says. "The first phase of clinical trials on humans started just eighteen months ago." I eye my mother, watching her nod eagerly, her short blond bob moving up and down at the doctor's words.

I wonder how many strings she had to pull and how much money she had to throw away to get me into this.

"We're monitoring him, but Will needs to help us. He

needs to keep the variables in his life to a minimum." Her eyes focus on me, her thin face serious. "Will. The risks of cross-infection are even higher now so—"

I cut her off. "Don't cough on any other CFers. Got it."

Her black eyebrows jut down as she frowns. "Don't get close enough to touch them. For their safety, and yours."

I hold up my hand in mock pledge, reciting what could probably be the CF motto by this point, "Six feet at all times."

She nods. "You got it."

"What I've got is B. cepacia, making this conversation null and void." That's not going to change anytime soon.

"Nothing is impossible!" Dr. Hamid says enthusiastically. My mom eats this line up. "I believe that. You need to believe it too."

I pair an over-the-top smile with a thumbs-up, before turning it into a thumbs-down and shaking my head, the smile slipping off my face. It's such bullshit.

Dr. Hamid clears her throat, looking at my mom. "Right. I'll leave this to you."

"Thank you, Dr. Hamid," my mom says, shaking her hand eagerly, like she just managed to sign a contract for her most burdensome client.

Dr. Hamid gives me a final thin-lipped smile before leaving. My mom spins around to look at me, her blue eyes piercing, voice biting. "It took a *lot* of effort to get you into this program, Will."

If by "effort" she means writing a check that could send a small village to college, then she definitely put in quite a bit of effort just so I could be a human petri dish.

"What do you want? A thank-you for shoving me in another hospital, wasting more of my time?" I stand up, walking over to face her. "In two weeks I'll be eighteen. A legal adult. You won't hold the reins anymore."

For a second she looks taken aback, then her eyes narrow at me. She grabs her latest Prada trench coat off the chair by the door, pulling it on and glancing back to look at me. "I'll see you on your birthday."

I lean out the doorway, watching her go, her heels clicking off down the hallway. She stops at the nurses' station, where Barb is flipping through some papers.

"Barb, right? Let me give you my cell," I hear her say as she opens her purse, grabbing her wallet from inside. "If the Cevaflomalin doesn't work, Will may . . . become a handful."

When Barb doesn't say anything, she pulls a business card out of her wallet. "He's been disappointed so many times already, and he's expecting to be disappointed again. If he's not complying, you'll call me?"

She flicks the business card onto the counter before tossing a hundred on top of it like this is some fancy restaurant and I'm a table that needs to be fawned over. Wow. That's just great.

Barb stares at the money, raising her eyebrows at my mother.

"That was inappropriate, wasn't it? I'm sorry. We've been to so many . . ."

Her voice trails off, and I watch as Barb takes the business card and the money off the counter, meeting my mother's gaze with the same look of determination she gives me when she's forcing me to take some medicine. "Don't worry. He's in good hands." She presses the hundred back into my mother's hand, pocketing the business card and looking past my mother to meet my eyes.

I duck back inside my room, closing the door behind me and tugging at the neck of my T-shirt. I pace over to the window, and then back over to sit down on my bed, and then back over to the window, pushing back the blinds as the walls start to close in on me.

I need to get outside. I need air that's not filled with antiseptic.

I throw open my closet door to grab a hoodie, pulling it on and peering out at the nurses' station to see if the coast is clear.

No sign of Barb or my mom anymore, but Julie's on the phone behind the desk, in between me and the exit door that will take me straight to the only stairwell in this building that leads to the roof.

I close my door quietly, creeping down the hall. I try to duck down lower than the nurses' station, but a six-foot dude attempting to stay low and sneak around is about as subtle as a blindfolded elephant. Julie looks up at me and I press my back up against the wall, pretending to camouflage myself. Her eyes narrow at me as she moves the phone away from her mouth. "Where do you think you're going?"

I mime walking with my fingers.

She shakes her head at me, knowing I've been confined to the third floor since I fell asleep by the vending machines over in Building 2 last week and caused a hospital-wide manhunt. I put my hands together, making a pleading motion and hoping the desperation pouring out of my soul will convince her otherwise.

At first, nothing. Her face remains firm, her gaze unchanging. Then she rolls her eyes, throwing me a face mask before waving me along to freedom.

Thank god. I need to get out of this whitewashed hell more than I need anything.

I give her a wink. At least she's actually human.

I leave the CF wing, pushing open the heavy door to the stairwell and taking the concrete steps by twos even though my lungs are burning after just one floor. Coughing, I pull at the metal railing, past the fourth floor, and the fifth, and then sixth, finally coming to a big red door with a huge notice stamped onto it: EMERGENCY EXIT. ALARM WILL SOUND WHEN DOOR IS OPENED.

I grab my wallet from my back pocket, taking out a tightly folded dollar that I keep in there for moments like these. I reach up and wedge the bill into the frame's alarm switch so the alarm doesn't go off, then I open the door just a crack and slide through onto the rooftop.

Then I bend down to put my wallet in between the door and the jamb so it doesn't slam shut behind me. I've learned that lesson the hard way before.

My mom would have a heart attack if she saw I was using the Louis Vuitton wallet she got me a few months ago as a doorstop, but it was a stupid gift to give someone who never goes anywhere but hospital cafeterias.

At least as a doorstop it gets used.

I stand up, taking a deep breath and automatically coughing as the cold, harsh winter air shocks my lungs. It feels good, though, to be outside. To not be trapped inside monochrome walls.

I stretch, looking up at the pale-gray sky, the predicted snowflakes finally drifting slowly through the air and landing on my cheeks and hair. I walk slowly to the roof's edge and take a seat on the icy stone, dangling my legs off the side. I exhale a breath I feel like I've been holding since I got here two weeks ago.

Everything's beautiful from up here.

No matter what hospital I go to, I always make it a point to find a way to get to the roof.

I've seen parades from the one in Brazil, the people looking like brightly colored ants as they danced through the streets, wild and free. I've seen France sleep, the Eiffel Tower shining brightly in the distance, lights quietly shutting off in third-floor apartments, the moon drifting lazily into view. I've seen the beaches in California, water that goes on for miles and miles, people basking in the perfect waves first thing in the morning.

Every place is different. Every place is unique. It's the hospitals I'm seeing them from that are the same.

This town isn't the life of the party, but it feels sort of back-roads homey. Maybe that should make me feel more comfortable, but it's only making me more restless. Probably because for the first time in eight months, I'm a car ride away from home. *Home.* Where Hope and Jason are. Where my old classmates are slowly chugging their way to finals, shooting for whatever Ivy League school their parents selected for them. Where my bedroom, my freaking life, really, sits empty and unlived in.

I watch the headlights of the cars driving past on the road next to the hospital, the twinkling holiday lights in the distance, the laughing kids sliding around on the icy pond next to a small park.

There's something simple in that. A freedom that makes my fingertips itch.

I remember when that used to be me and Jason, sliding around on the icy pond down the street from his house, the cold sinking deep into our bones as we played. We'd be out there for hours, having contests to see who could slide farther without falling, chucking snowballs at each other, making snow angels.

We made the most of every minute until my mom inevitably showed up and dragged me back inside.

The lights flick on in the hospital courtyard, and I glance down to see a girl sitting inside her room on the third floor, typing away on a laptop, a pair of headphones sitting overtop her ears as she concentrates on her screen.

Wait a second.

I squint. Stella.

The cold wind tugs at my hair, and I put my hood up, watching her face as she types.

What could she possibly be working on? It's a Saturday night.

She was so different in the videos I watched. I wonder what changed. Is it all of this? All of the hospital stuff? The pills and the treatments and those whitewashed walls that push in on you and suffocate you slowly, day by day.

I stand up, balancing on the edge of the roof, and peer at the courtyard seven stories down, just for a moment imagining the weightlessness, the absolute abandon of the fall. I see Stella look up through the glass and we make eye contact just as a strong gust of wind knocks the air right out of me. I try to take a breath to get it back, but my shitty lungs barely take in any oxygen.

What air I do get catches in my throat and I start to cough. *Hard.*

My rib cage screams as each cough pulls more and more air from my lungs, my eyes starting to water.

Finally, I start to get control of it, but—

My head swims, the edges of my vision going black.

I stumble, freaked out, whipping my head around and trying to focus on the red exit door or the ground or *anything*. I stare at my hands, willing the black to clear away, the world to come back into view, knowing the open air over the edge of the roof is still barely an inch away.

CHAPTER 5

STELLA

I slam open the door to the stairwell, buttoning my jacket as I book it up the steps to the roof. My heart is pounding so loud in my ears, I can barely hear my footsteps underneath me as I run up the steps.

He has to be crazy.

I keep picturing him standing there at the edge of the roof, about to plummet seven stories to his death, fear painted onto every feature of his face. Nothing like his previous confident smirk.

Wheezing, I make it past the fifth floor, stopping just a moment to catch my breath, my sweaty palms grabbing at the cool metal railing. I peer up the stairwell to the top floor, my head spinning, my sore throat burning. I didn't even have time to grab my portable oxygen. Just two more stories. Two more. I force myself to keep climbing, my feet moving on command: right, left, right, left, right, left.

Finally the door to the roof is in sight, cracked open under a bright red alarm just *ready* to go off.

I hesitate, looking from the alarm to the door and back again. But why didn't it go off when Will opened it? Is it broken?

Then I see it. A folded dollar bill holding down the switch, stopping the alarm from blaring and letting everyone in the hospital know some crazy guy with cystic fibrosis and self-destructive tendencies is hanging out on the roof.

I shake my head. He might be crazy, but that's clever.

The door is propped open with a wallet, and I push through it as quickly as I can, making sure the dollar bill stays securely in place over the switch. I stop dead, catching a real breath for the first time in forty-eight stairs. Looking across the roof, I'm relieved to see he's moved a safe distance away from the edge and hasn't fallen to his death. He turns to look at me as I wheeze, a surprised expression on his face. I pull my red scarf closer as the cold air bites at my face and neck, looking down to see if his wallet is still wedged in the doorjamb before storming over to him.

"Do you have a death wish?" I shout, stopping a more-than-safe eight feet away from him. He may have one, but I certainly don't.

His cheeks and nose are red from the cold, and a thin layer of snow has collected on his wavy brown hair and the hood of his burgundy sweatshirt. When he looks like that, I can almost pretend he's not such an idiot.

But then he starts talking again.

He shrugs at me, casually, motioning over the edge of the roof to the ground below. "My lungs are toast. So I'm going to enjoy the view while I can."

How poetic.

Why did I expect anything different?

I peer past him to see the twinkling city skyline far, far in the distance, the holiday lights covering every inch of every tree, brighter now than I've ever seen them as they bring the park below back to life. Some are even strung across the trees, creating this magical pathway you could walk under, head back, mouth agape.

In all my years here I've never been on the roof. Shivering, I pull my jacket tighter, wrapping my arms around my body as I move my eyes back to him.

"Good view or not, why would anyone want to risk falling seven stories?" I ask him, genuinely wondering what would possess someone with defective lungs to take a trip onto the roof in the dead of winter.

His blue eyes light up in a way that makes my stomach flip-flop. "You ever see Paris from a roof, Stella? Or Rome? Or here, even? It's the only thing that makes all this treatment crap seem small."

"'Treatment crap'?" I ask, taking two steps toward him. Six feet apart. The limit. "That treatment crap is what keeps us alive."

He snorts, rolling his eyes. "That treatment crap is what

stops us from being down there and actually living."

My blood begins to boil. "Do you even know how lucky you are to be in this drug trial? But you just take it for granted. A spoiled, privileged brat."

"Wait, how do you know about the trial? You been asking about me?"

I ignore his questions, pushing on. "If you don't care, then leave," I fire back. "Let someone else take your spot in the trial. Someone who wants to live."

I look up at him, watching as the snow falls in the space between us, disappearing as it lands in the dusting under our feet. We stare at each other in silence, and then he shrugs, his expression unreadable. He takes a step backward, toward the edge again. "You're right. I mean, I'm dying anyway."

I narrow my eyes at him. He wouldn't. Right?

Another step back. And another, his footsteps crunching in the freshly fallen snow. His eyes are locked on mine, daring me to say something, to stop him. Challenging me to call out to him.

Closer. Almost to the edge.

I inhale sharply, the cold scraping at the inside of my lungs.

He dangles one foot off the end, and the open air makes my throat tighten up. He can't— "Will! No! Stop!" I shout, taking a step closer to him, my heart pounding in my ears.

He stops, leg floating off the edge. One more step and he would have fallen. One more step and he would have . . .

We stare at each other in silence, his blue eyes curious,

interested. And then he starts to laugh, loud and deep and wild, in a way so familiar, it feels like pressing on a bruise.

"Oh my god. The look on your face was priceless." He mimics my voice, "Will! No! Stop!"

"Are you fucking kidding me? Why would you do that? Falling to your death isn't a joke!" I can feel my whole body shaking. I dig my fingernails into my palm, trying to stop the trembling as I turn away from him.

"Oh, come on, Stella!" he calls after me. "I was only fooling around."

I pull open the rooftop door and step over the wallet, wanting to put as much space as possible between us. Why did I even bother? Why did I climb four stories to see if he was okay? I start running down the first few steps, reaching up to realize . . . I forgot to put on my face mask.

I never forget my face mask.

I slow down and then stop completely as an idea pops into my head. Climbing back up to the door, I slowly pull the dollar bill off the alarm switch, pocketing it as I fly back down to the third floor of the hospital.

Leaning against the brick wall, I catch my breath before pulling off my jacket and scarf, opening the door, and strolling to my room, as if I've just been off at the NICU. Somewhere in the distance, the roof alarm goes off as Will opens the door to get back inside, distant but blaring as it echoes down the stairwell, reverberating in the hallway.

I can't help but smile.

Julie tosses a blue patient folder onto the desk behind the nurses' station, shaking her head and murmuring to herself, "The roof, Will? Really?"

Good to know I'm not the only one he's driving crazy.

I gaze out the window, watching the snow fall in the fluorescent glow of the courtyard lights, the hallway finally dead silent after Will's hour-long reprimanding. Glancing over at the clock, I see it's only eight p.m., which gives me plenty of time to work on number 14 on my to-do list, "Prepare app for beta testing," and number 15, "Complete dosage table for diabetes," before I go to bed tonight.

I check my Facebook quickly before getting started, a red notification for an invite to a Senior Trip Beach Blast this Friday night in Cabo popping up. I click on the page and see that they used the description I'd drafted back when I was still organizing this, and I'm not sure if that makes me feel better or worse. I scroll through the list of people going, seeing Camila's and Mya's pictures, and Mason's (now sans Brooke), followed by pictures of a half dozen other people from my school who have already replied with a yes.

My iPad begins to ring, and I see a FaceTime call coming in from Camila. It's like they knew I was thinking about them. I smile and swipe right to accept the call, almost getting blinded when the bright sunshine of whatever pristine beach they're sitting on bursts through the screen of my iPad.

"Okay, I'm officially jealous!" I say as Camila's sunburnt face comes into view.

Mya lunges to stick her face over Camila's shoulder, her curly hair bouncing into the frame. She's wearing the polka-dot one-piece I helped her pick out, but she clearly doesn't have time for pleasantries. "Are there any cute guys there? And don't you dare say—"

"Just Poe," we say at the same time.

Camila shrugs, fixing her glasses. "Poe counts. He is CUTE!"

Mya snorts, nudging Camila. "Poe is a thousand percent not interested in you, Camila."

Camila punches her playfully in the arm, and then freezes, squinting at me. "Oh my god. Is there? Stella, is there a cute guy there?"

I roll my eyes. "He is *not* cute."

"'He'!" The two of them squeal in delight, and I can sense the waterfall of questions that's about to pour over me.

"I gotta go! Talk to you tomorrow!" I say while they protest, and hang up. The moment on the roof is still a little too fresh and weird to talk about. The page for the Cabo beach party swings back into view. I hover over "Not Going" but I can't bring myself to click on it just yet, so instead I just close the page and pull up Visual Studio.

I open the project I've been working on and begin to sort

through the lines and lines of code, already feeling my muscles loosen as I do. I find an error in line 27, where I put a *c* instead of an *x* for a variable, and a missing equal sign in line 182, but aside from that, the app finally looks ready to go for beta. I almost can't believe it. I'll celebrate with a pudding cup later.

I try to move on to completing the dosage table for diabetes in my spreadsheet of the most prevalent chronic conditions, sorting through varying ages and weights and medications. But I soon find myself staring at the blank columns, my fingertips tapping away at the edge of my laptop instead, my mind a million miles away.

Focus.

I reach over to grab my pocket notebook, crossing off number 14 and trying to get the feeling of calm that usually comes from finishing to-do list items, but it doesn't come. I freeze as my pencil hovers over number 15, looking from the blank columns and rows on my spreadsheet back down to "Complete dosage table for diabetes."

Unfinished. Ugh.

I chuck the notebook onto my bed, restlessness and unease filling my stomach. Standing up, I walk over to the window, my hand pushing back the blinds.

My eyes travel to the roof, to the spot where Will was standing earlier. I know he was his usual self when I got up there, but I didn't imagine the coughing, and teetering. Or the fear.

Mr. "Death Comes for Us All" didn't want to die.

Restless, I walk over to my med cart, hoping that moving on to "Before-bed meds" on my to-do list will help calm me down. My fingers tap away on the metal of the cart as I look at the sea of bottles, and then out the window again at the roof, and then back at the bottles.

Is he even doing his treatments?

Barb can probably force him to take most of his meds, but she can't be there for every single dose. She can strap him into his AffloVest, but she can't ensure he keeps it on for the full half hour.

He's probably not doing all his treatments.

I try to go over the meds in order of when I take them, shuffling them around on the cart, the names all blurring together. Instead of feeling calm, I feel more and more frustration, the anger climbing up the sides of my head.

I struggle with the cap on a mucus thinner, pressing down on it with all my strength and trying to twist it off.

I don't want him to die.

The thought climbs on top of the mountain of frustration and plants a flag, clear and loud and so surprising to me that I don't even understand it. I just see him walking back to the edge of that roof. And even though he's the actual worst . . .

I don't want him to die.

I twist the lid sharply and it comes flying off, pills showering down onto my med cart. Angrily, I slam the bottle down, the pills jumping again with the force of my hand. "Dammit!"

CHAPTER 6

WILL

I open the door to MY ROOM, surprised to see Stella backing up against the wall on the other side of the hallway. After the stunt I pulled yesterday, I thought she'd steer clear of me for at LEAST a week. She's wearing about four face masks and two pairs of gloves, her fingers wrapping tightly around the plastic handrail on the wall. As she moves, I catch the scent of lavender.

It smells nice. It's probably my nose craving anything that isn't bleach.

I grin. "Are you my proctologist?"

She gives me what I think is an icy look from what I can see of her face, leaning to peer past me into my room. I glance behind me to see what she's looking at. The art books, the AffloVest hanging on the edge of the bed from when I shrugged it off as soon as Barb left, my open sketchbook on the table. That's about it.

"I knew it," she says finally, like she confirmed the answer to some great Sherlock Holmes mystery. She holds out her double-gloved hand. "Let me see your regimen."

"You're kidding, right?"

We stare each other down, her brown eyes shooting daggers through me while I try to give her an equally intimidating glare. But I'm bored as shit so my curiosity gets the better of me. I roll my eyes and turn to go rip apart my room looking for a sheet of paper that's probably already in a landfill somewhere.

I push aside some magazines and check under the bed. I riffle through a couple of my sketchbook pages, and even look under my pillow for show, but it's nowhere to be found.

I straighten up and shake my head at her. "Can't find it. Sorry. See ya later."

She doesn't budge, though, and crosses her arms in defiance, refusing to leave.

So I keep looking, my eyes scanning the room while Stella taps her foot in the hallway impatiently. It's useless. That thing is—wait.

I notice my pocket-size sketchbook lying on my dresser, the regimen crammed into the back of it, neatly folded and just barely sticking out past the small pages of the book.

My mom must have hidden it there so it didn't end up in the garbage bin.

I grab it, heading back to the doorway, and hold out the paper to her. "Not that it's any of your business . . ."

She snatches the paper from me before pressing back up against the far wall. I see her furiously looking at the neat columns and rows that I made into a pretty sick cartoon, imitating a level of Donkey Kong, while Mom and Dr. Hamid chatted. The ladders sit on top of my dosage information, rolling barrels bounce around my treatment names, the damsel in distress screams "HELP!" in the left-hand corner next to my name. Clever, right?

"What is—how could you—why?"

Clearly, she doesn't think so.

"Is this what an aneurysm looks like? Should I call Julie?"

She shoves the paper back at me, her face like thunder.

"Hey," I say, holding up my hands. "I get that you have some save-the-world hero complex going on, but leave me out of it."

She shakes her head at me. "Will. These treatments aren't optional. These *meds* aren't optional."

"Which is probably why they keep shoving them down my throat." To be fair, though, anything can be optional if you're creative enough.

Stella shakes her head, throwing up her hands and storming off down the hallway. "You're making me crazy!"

Dr. Hamid's words from earlier surprise me by playing through my head. *Don't get close enough to touch them. For their safety, and yours.* I grab a face mask from an unopened box of them that Julie put by my door, pocket it, and jog after her.

I glance to the side to see a short, brown-haired boy with a sharp nose, and even sharper cheekbones, peering out of room 310, his eyebrows raised curiously at me as I follow Stella down the hall to the elevator. She reaches the elevator first, stepping inside and turning to face me as she hits the floor button. I move to step in after her but she holds up her hand.

"Six feet."

Shit.

The doors slide shut and I tap my foot impatiently, pressing the up button over and over and over again as I watch the elevator climb steadily up to the fifth floor and then slowly back down to me. I glance nervously at the empty nurses' station behind me before sliding quickly into the elevator and jamming the door-close button. I meet my own gaze in the blurry metal of the elevator, remembering the face mask in my pocket and slinging it on as I ride up to the fifth floor. This is stupid. Why am I even following Barb Jr.?

With a ding, the door slowly opens, and I power walk down the hall and across the bridge to the east entrance of the NICU, dodging a few doctors along the way. They're all clearly on their way somewhere, so no one stops me. Gently pushing open the door, I watch Stella for a moment. I open my mouth to ask what the hell that was all about, but then I see that her expression is dark. Serious. I stop a safe distance away from her and follow her eyes to the baby, more tubes and wires than limbs.

I see the tiny chest, struggling to rise and fall, struggling to continue breathing. I feel my own heartbeat in my chest, my own weak lungs trying to fill with air from my mad dash through the hospital.

"She's fighting for her life," she finally says, meeting my eyes in the glass. "She doesn't know what's ahead of her or why she's fighting. It's just . . . instinct, Will. Her instinct is to fight. To live."

Instinct.

I lost that instinct a long time ago. Maybe at my fiftieth hospital, in Berlin. Maybe about eight months ago when I contracted B. cepacia and they ripped my name off the transplant list. There are a lot of possibilities.

My jaw tightens. "Listen, you've got the wrong guy for that inspiring little speech—"

"Please." She cuts me off, spinning around to face me with a surprising amount of desperation in her expression. "I need you to follow your regimen. Strictly and completely."

"I don't think I heard that right. Did you just say . . . please?" I say, trying to dodge the seriousness of this conversation. Her expression doesn't change, though. I shake my head, stepping closer to her but not too close. Something's up.

"Okay. What's really going on here? I won't laugh."

She takes a deep breath, taking two steps back to my one step forward. "I have . . . control issues. I need to know that things are in order."

"So? What does that have to do with me?"

"I know you're not doing your treatments." She leans against the glass, looking at me. "And it's messing me up. Bad."

I clear my throat, looking past her at the small, helpless baby on the other side of the glass. I feel a twinge of guilt, even though that makes no sense.

"Yeah, well, I'd love to help you out. But what you're asking . . ." I shake my head, shrugging. "Eh, I don't know how."

"Bullshit, Will," she says, stomping her foot. "All CFers know how to administer their own treatments. We're practically doctors by the time we're twelve."

"Even us spoiled, privileged brats?" I challenge, ripping the face mask off. She isn't amused by my comment, and her face is still frustrated, distressed. I don't know what the real problem is, but it's clearly eating away at her. This is more than control issues. Taking a deep breath, I stop screwing around. "You're serious? I'm messing you up?"

She doesn't respond, and we stand there, staring at each other in silence, something bordering on understanding passing between us. Finally, I take a step back and put on the face mask again as a peace offering, before leaning against the wall. "Okay. All right," I say, eyeing her. "So, if I agree to this, what's in it for me?"

Her eyes narrow and she pulls her heather-gray hoodie closer to her. I watch her, the way her hair falls over her shoulders, the way her eyes show every little thing she's feeling.

"I want to draw you," I say before I can stop myself.

"What?" she says, shaking her head adamantly. "No."

"Why not?" I ask. "You're beautiful."

Shit. That slipped out. She stares at me, surprised and, unless I'm imagining it, just a little pleased. "Thank you, but no way."

I shrug and start walking toward the door. "Guess we don't have a deal."

"You can't practice a little discipline? Stick to your regimen? Even to save your own life?"

I stop short, looking back at her. She doesn't get it. "*Nothing*'s gonna save my life, Stella. Or yours." I keep going down the hallway, calling over my shoulder, "Everyone in this world is breathing borrowed air."

I push the door open and am about to leave when her voice rings out from behind me.

"Ugh, fine!"

I spin around, shocked, the door clicking shut.

"But no nudes," she adds. She's taken her face mask off and I can see her lips twitching into a smile. The first one she's given me. She's making a joke.

Stella Grant is making a joke.

I laugh, shaking my head. "Ah, I should've known you'd find a way to suck all the fun out of it."

"No posing for hours on end," she says, looking back at the

preemie, her face suddenly serious. "And your regimen. We do it my way."

"Deal," I say, knowing that whatever she means by her way is going to be a gigantic pain in the ass. "I'd say let's shake on it, but . . ."

"Funny," she says, looking at me and then nodding toward the door. "The first thing you have to do is get a med cart in your room."

I salute. "On it. Med cart in my room."

I push open the door, giving her a big smile that lasts me all the way back to the elevator. Pulling out my phone, I send a quick text to Jason: Get this, dude: a truce with that girl I told you about.

He's been getting a real kick out of the stories I've been telling him about her. He cried from laughing over the door alarm incident yesterday.

My phone buzzes with his reply as the elevator slows to a stop on the third floor: Must be your good looks. Clearly not because of your charming personality.

Pocketing my phone, I peer around the corner to check that the nurses' station is still empty before sliding off the elevator. I jump when a loud crash reverberates out from an open door.

"Ow. Shit," a voice says from inside.

I peek in to see the dark-haired dude from earlier wearing a pair of flannel pajama pants and a Food Network T-shirt.

He's sitting on the floor next to an overturned skateboard, rubbing his elbow, clearly post-wipeout.

"Oh, hey," he says, standing up and picking up the skateboard. "You just missed the show."

"You doing stunts in here?"

He shrugs. "No safer place to break a leg. Besides, Barb just went off shift."

Valid point. "Can't argue with logic." I laugh, raising my hand to do a small wave. "I'm Will."

"Poe," he says, grinning back at me.

We grab chairs out of our rooms and sit in our respective doorways. It's nice to talk to someone around here who's not mad at me all the time.

"So what brings you to Saint Grace's? Haven't seen you here before. Stell and I pretty much know everyone who comes through."

Stell. So they're close?

I lean my chair back, letting it rest against the doorframe, and try to drop the B. cepacia bomb as casually as I can. "Experimental trial for B. cepacia."

I usually avoid telling CFers because they make it a point to avoid me like the plague.

His eyes widen, but he doesn't move any farther away. He just rolls the skateboard back and forth under his feet. "B. cepacia? That is *rough.* How long ago did you contract it?"

"About eight months ago," I say. I remember waking up

one morning having more trouble breathing than usual, and then I couldn't stop coughing. My mom, being obsessed with every breath I've taken my whole life, took me straight to the hospital to run some tests. I can still hear her heels clicking loudly behind the gurney, her ordering the people around as if she were the chief of surgery.

I thought she was obsessive before the results came back. She always overreacted to every loud cough or gasp of breath, keeping me out of school or forcing me to cancel plans to go to doctor's appointments or to the hospital for no reason.

I remember doing a mandatory chorus performance back in third grade and coughing right in the middle of our shitty rendition of "This Little Light of Mine." She literally stopped the concert midsong and dragged me offstage to go get a checkup.

But I didn't know how good I had it. Things are so much worse now than they were then. Hospital after hospital, experimental trial after experimental trial. Every week it's another attempt to fix the problem, cure the incurable. A minute without an IV or not talking about a next step is a minute wasted.

But nothing is going to get me back on a lung transplant list. And every week we waste, more of my lung function wastes away too.

"It colonized so freakin' fast," I tell Poe, putting the front legs of my chair back on the ground. "One minute I was at the top of the transplant list, and then one throat culture later . . ." I clear my throat, trying not to let the disappointment show, and shrug. "Whatever."

No sense dwelling on what could've been.

Poe snorts. "Well, I am *sure* that attitude"—he mimics my shrug and hair flip— "is what's driving Stella crazy."

"Sounds like you know her well. What's that about, anyway? She said she's just a control freak, but . . ."

"Call it whatever you want, but Stella's got her shit together." He stops rolling the skateboard and gives me a big smile. "She definitely keeps me in line."

"She's bossy."

"Nah, she's a boss," Poe says, and I can tell from the expression on his face that he means it. "She's seen me through thick and thin, man."

Now I'm curious. I narrow my eyes. "Have you guys ever . . . ?"

"Hooked up?" Poe says, tilting his head back to laugh. "Oh, man. No way! No. No. No."

I give him a look. She's cute. And he clearly cares about her. A lot. I find it hard to believe that he never even *tried* to make a move.

"I mean, for one thing, we're both CFers. No touching," he says. This time he's giving *me* the calculated look. "Sex isn't worth dying for, if you ask me."

I snort, shaking my head. Clearly, everyone on this wing has just had "fine" sex. For some reason, everyone thinks that if you've got a disease or a disorder or are sick, you become a saint.

Which is a crock of shit.

CF might actually have improved my sex life, if anything. Besides, the one perk of moving around so much is that I don't stay anywhere long enough to catch feelings. Jason seems pretty happy since he got all sappy with Hope, but I don't really need more serious shit in my life.

"Second, she's been my best friend practically my whole life," he says, bringing me back to the present. I swear he's getting a little teary eyed.

"I think you love her," I say, teasing him.

"Oh, hell yeah. I fucking adore her," Poe says like it's a no-brainer. "Would lie down on hot coals for her. I'd give her my lungs if they were worth a shit."

Damn. I try to ignore the jealousy that swims into my chest.

"Then I don't get it. Why—"

"She is not a *he*," Poe says, cutting me off.

It takes a second for the penny to drop, but then I laugh, shaking my head. "Way to bury the lead, dude."

I'm not sure why I'm so relieved, but I am. I stare at the dry-erase board hanging on the door directly above his head, noticing a big heart drawn on it.

If Stella's trying to keep me alive too, she must not *completely* hate me, right?

CHAPTER 7

STELLA

"Just give me ten minutes," I say, shutting the door and leaving Will and Poe out in the hallway.

I look around his room as my app downloads onto his phone, seeing the note I slipped under his door this morning sitting on top of his bed.

"Text me when you have the med cart. (718) 555 3295. I will be over this afternoon to set everything up."

I knew that one would be tricky, especially because Will and Barb are clearly not on the best of terms, so she wouldn't advocate for him, but he went above her head and managed to charm Dr. Hamid. I pick up the note, noticing he's drawn a tiny cartoon along the edge, of an angry Barb in her signature colorful scrubs, pushing a med cart and screaming, "DON'T MAKE ME REGRET THIS!"

I shake my head, a smile slipping onto my lips as I put the note back down and walk over to the actual med cart. I rearrange a few pill bottles, making sure one more time that everything is in the same chronological order as what I programmed into the app after cross-referencing his Donkey Kong–covered regimen.

I double-check his laptop to see how much longer for the download to be complete from the link I sent him, trying not to breathe more than I have to in this B. cepacia–laden room.

Eighty-eight percent complete.

My heart jumps as I hear noise outside the doorway, and I yank my hand away from the keyboard, worried we've been caught. *Please don't be Barb. Please don't be Barb.* She should be on her lunch break, but if she's back already, getting a jump on her Monday-afternoon rounds, she'll murder me.

Will's footsteps echo back and forth, back and forth, in front of the doorway, and I tiptoe to the door, almost pressing my ear up against it. But I'm relieved to hear only the two of their voices.

"You wiped everything down, right?" Poe says.

"Of course I did. Twice, just to be safe," Will shoots back. "I mean, clearly, this wasn't my idea, you know."

I adjust the isolation gown over the top of my disposable scrubs, and yank open the door, squinting at them through my goggles.

Poe spins around on his skateboard to face me. "Man, Stella. Did I tell you how fiiine you look today?"

He and Will break out into laughter for the third time

over my makeshift hazmat suit. I glare at them before glancing down the hallway.

"Still clear?"

He pushes off on his skateboard and slowly rolls past the nurses' station, peering over the desk.

He shoots a thumbs-up in my direction. "Just hurry up."

"I'm almost done!" I say, ducking back into the room and closing the door.

I eye the med cart, breathing a sigh of contentment over how meticulously organized it is. But then I see the desk his laptop is sitting on, which is so . . . not. I march over and grab a handful of colored pencils, putting them safely back in the pencil holder they belong in. I straighten up the magazines and sketchbooks, making sure they are in order by size, and as I do, a piece of paper falls out.

It's a cartoon boy who looks a lot like Will holding a pair of balloons and forcing air into deflated-looking lungs, his face red from the effort. I grin, reading the caption under it: "Just breathe."

It's really good.

Reaching out, I gently trace Will's lungs, like I do with Abby's drawing. My gloved fingertips land on the small cartoon of Will, his sharp jawline, his unruly hair, his blue eyes, and the same burgundy sweatshirt he was wearing on the roof.

All that's missing is the smile.

I look up at the wall, noticing he has only an old cartoon

hung up right above his bed. Grabbing a tack from a small jar, I hang his cartoon on the wall below it.

The laptop dings and I blink, quickly pulling my hand away. Upload complete. I spin around, walking to his desk and unplugging his phone. Scooping everything up, I pull open the door and hold out the phone to the noncartoon Will.

He stretches to take it from me, fixing his face mask with the other hand.

"I built an app for chronic illnesses. Med charts, schedules." I shrug casually. "It'll alert you when you need to take your pills or do a treat—"

"You *built* an app? Like, built it, built it?" he cuts me off, looking from the phone to me in surprise, his blue eyes wide.

"Newsflash. Girls can code."

His phone chirps and I see the animated pill bottle appear on his screen. "Ivacaftor. A hundred and fifty milligrams," I tell him. Damn, I already feel better.

I raise my eyebrows at Will, who is giving me a look that's not mocking for once. He's impressed. Good. "My app is so simple even boys can figure it out."

I saunter off, swaying my nonexistent hips confidently, cheeks warm as I head straight to the public bathroom on the other side of the floor that no one uses.

The light flickers on as I lock the door behind me. I rip off my gloves and grab some disinfectant wipes from a round bin by the door, scrubbing my hands down three times. Exhaling slowly, I rip everything I'm wearing off; the booties and the cap and the face mask and the scrubs and the gown. I shove them all into the bin, pushing them down and closing the lid before running to the sink.

My skin is crawling, like I can feel the B. cepacia looking for a way to slip inside and eat away at me.

I go to the sink and turn the handle, hot water pouring loudly out of the tap. I grip the smooth porcelain, looking at myself in the mirror, standing there in my bra and underwear. The handful of raised scars lining my chest and stomach from surgery after surgery, my ribs pushing through my skin when I breathe, the sharp angle of my collarbone made sharper by the dim lighting of the bathroom. The redness around my G-tube is worsening, an infection definitely starting to form.

I'm too thin, too scarred, too . . . I meet my hazel eyes in the mirror.

Why would Will want to draw me?

His voice echoes in my head, calling me beautiful. *Beautiful.* It makes my heart flip in a way it shouldn't.

Steam begins to cloud the mirror, blurring the image. I look away, pumping the soap until it overflows in my hand. I scrub my hands and my arms and my face with it, washing everything away and down the sink. Then I apply some heavy-duty hand sanitizer for good measure.

I dry off, opening the lid on the second trash can and pulling out a bag of clothes that I carefully put there an hour earlier on my way to Will's room. Once I'm dressed, I glance in the mirror one more time before carefully leaving the bathroom, making sure no one sees me exiting. Good as new.

Lounging on my bed, I eye my Monday to-do list warily but keep scrolling through social media on my phone instead. I tap on Camila's Instagram Story, watching for the millionth time as she waves happily to the camera from a kayak, holding the phone over her head to show Mya paddling frantically behind her.

Most of my time since the secret hazmat operation has been spent vicariously absorbing Cabo through my classmates' Instagram Stories. I went snorkeling in crystal-blue waters with Melissa. Sailing with Jude to see the Arch of Cabo San Lucas. Basked on the beach with a seemingly not-too-heartbroken Brooke.

Just as I'm about to hit refresh yet again, there's a knock on my door and Barb pops her head in. She eyes my med cart for a second and I'm pretty sure I know what's coming. "Have you been in Will's room? His setup looks . . . awful familiar."

I shake my head, nope. Wasn't me. A perk of being a goody two shoes is that Barb will probably believe me.

I'm relieved when my laptop dings with a FaceTime notification, Poe's picture popping up on the screen. I freeze before answering it, silently willing him not to say anything about Will as I spin my laptop around.

"Look who just got back from lunch break!"

Luckily, his eyes immediately travel over to see Barb standing in the doorway, and he holds back whatever comments he's about to make.

"Oh. Hey, Barb." He clears his throat. Barb smiles at him as he starts rambling on about pears flambé with some kind of reduction. I watch as she slowly closes the door, my heart pounding in my ears until I hear the gentle click of the latch sliding into place.

I exhale slowly as Poe gives me a look.

"Listen. I get what you're doing. It's nice." He looks right into my freaking soul as usual. "But this thing with Will. Is it really the best idea? I mean, you of all people know better."

I shrug, because he's right. I do know better, don't I? But I also know more than anyone how to be careful. "It's only a couple of weeks, then I'm out of here. He can quit his treatment then for all I care."

He raises his eyebrows at me, smirking. "Senate-level dodge. Nicely done."

He thinks I'm *crushing* on Will. Crushing on the most sarcastic and annoying, not to mention infectious, boy I've ever met.

Time to change the subject.

"I'm not dodging anything!" I say. "That's your move."

"What's that supposed to mean?" he asks, narrowing his eyes at me because he knows full well.

"Ask Michael," I shoot back.

He ignores me and changes the topic right back. *"Please* don't tell me that the one time you're finally interested in a guy, he's a CFer."

"I just helped him with his med cart, Poe! Wanting someone to live isn't the same thing as wanting them," I say, exasperated.

I am not *interested* in Will. I don't have a death wish. And if I wanted to date an asshole, there are plenty without CF to choose from. It's ridiculous.

Isn't it?

"I know you, Stella. Organizing a med cart is like foreplay."

He studies my face, trying to see if I'm lying. I roll my eyes and slam the laptop shut before either of us can figure out if I am.

"They're called manners!" I hear Poe's annoyed voice shout down the hallway to me, followed by the sound of his door slamming shut a few seconds later.

My phone vibrates and I pick it up to see a text from Will.

Lovers' spat?

My stomach flips again, but I wrinkle my nose, about to delete the message, and then the four o'clock reminder for the AffloVest pops onto my screen, a tiny animated pill bottle dancing. I bite my lip, knowing Will just got the same notification. But will he follow through?

CHAPTER 8

WILL

I carefully shade Barb's hair, leaning back to look at the drawing I did of her holding a pitchfork. As I'm nodding in contentment, my phone begins vibrating noisily on my desk, making the colored pencils dance. It's Stella. On FaceTime.

Surprised, I reach over to pause the Pink Floyd song on my computer, swiping right to answer the call.

"I knew it!" she says as her wide eyes come into view. "Where's your AffloVest? You weren't supposed to take it off for another fifteen minutes. And did you take your Creon? I'll bet that's a no."

I fake an automated voice. "We're sorry, you have reached a number that is no longer in service. If you feel you have reached this recording in error—"

"You can't be trusted," she says, cutting into my killer impression. "So, here's how this is going to work. We'll do our treatments together so I know you're really doing them."

I tuck the pencil I was using behind my ear, playing it cool. "Always looking for ways to spend more time with me."

She hangs up, but for just a second I swear I saw her smile. Interesting.

We stay on Skype for most of the next two days, and surprisingly it's not all barking orders. She shows me her technique for taking pills with chocolate pudding. Which is freaking genius. And delicious. We breathe in our nebulizers, and do our IV drips, and mark off treatments and meds together in her app. But Stella was right a few days ago. For some reason me doing my treatments is helping her to relax. Gradually she's becoming less and less uptight.

And, I won't lie, even after two days, it's way easier to get out of bed in the morning. I'm for sure breathing better.

On the afternoon of the second day, I start to put on my AffloVest, jumping in surprise when Barb busts through the door, ready for the usual four o'clock fight that we have over it. She always wins the brawl to get it on after threatening to confine me in isolation, but that doesn't stop me from trying to get out of it.

I slam my laptop down, abruptly ending my Skype call with Stella as Barb and I stare at each other in a classic Old Western standoff. She looks from the AffloVest to me, the steel in her face melting away into a shocked expression.

"I don't believe my eyes. You're putting on your AffloVest."

I shrug like it's no big deal, glancing at the compressor to double-check that everything is hooked up right. It looks fine to me, but it's definitely been a while since I've done this myself. "It's four o'clock, isn't it?"

She rolls her eyes and pins me with a look.

"Leave it on for the whole time," she says, before sliding out the door.

The door is barely closed before I fling my laptop open, calling Stella on Skype as I lie upside down off my bed, pink bedpan in one hand for mucus disposal.

"Hey, sorry about that. Barb . . . ," I start to say when she picks up, my voice trailing off when I notice the dejected expression on her face, her full lips turning down into a frown as she stares at her phone. "You okay?"

"Yeah," she says, looking up at me and taking a deep breath. "My entire class is in Cabo for our school's senior trip." She turns her phone around to show me an Instagram picture of a group of people wearing bathing suits, and sunglasses, and hats, posing happily on a sandy beach.

She shrugs, putting her phone down. I can hear her vest vibrating through the computer, the steady hum in time with mine. "I'm just a little bummed I'm not there."

"I get that," I say, thinking of Jason and Hope and all that I've missed out on these past few months, living vicariously through their texts and social media feeds.

"I planned the whole thing this year too," she says, which

doesn't surprise me. She's probably planned every step she's ever taken.

"And your parents? They'd let you go?" I ask, curious. Even before the B. cepacia, my mom would've axed the idea. Vacations from school have always been needle times for me.

She nods, curiosity filling her eyes at my question. "Of course. If I was healthy enough. Wouldn't yours?"

"Nah, unless, of course, a hospital there is claiming to have some new magical stem-cell therapy to cure B. cepacia." I sit up and cough a whole bunch of mucus into my bedpan. Grimacing, I lie back down. I remember why I kept taking this off before it could really get going. "Besides, I've already been. It's beautiful there."

"You've been? What was it like?" she asks eagerly, pulling the laptop closer.

The blurry memory swims into focus, and I can see my dad standing next to me on the beach, the tide pulling at our feet, our toes digging into the sand. "Yeah, I went with my dad when I was little, before he left." I'm too caught up in the memory to process what I'm saying, but the word "dad" feels weird on my tongue.

Why did I tell her that? I never tell anyone that. I don't think I've even mentioned my dad in years.

She opens her mouth to say something, but I quickly change the subject back to Cabo's scenery. This isn't about him. "The beaches are nice. The water is crystal clear. Plus, everyone is super, super friendly and chill."

I see the dejection in her eyes growing over my rousing review, so I throw in a random fact I heard on the Travel Channel. "Oh, man, but the currents are so strong there! You almost never get a chance to swim, except for maybe, like, an hour or two every day. You just broil on the beach most of the time, since you can't go in the water."

"Really?" she asks, looking skeptical but grateful at my attempt.

I nod eagerly, watching as some of the sadness slides off her face.

We vibrate away, a comfortable silence settling over us. Except, of course, for the occasional hacking up of a lung.

After we finish using our AffloVests, Stella hangs up to give her mom a call and to check in on her friends in Cabo, vowing to call me back in time for our nighttime pills. The hours pass slowly without her smiling face on the other side of my computer screen. I eat dinner and draw and watch You-Tube videos, just like I used to do to kill time pre–Stella's intervention, but it all feels extra boring now. No matter what I do, I catch myself glancing over at my computer screen, waiting for the Skype call to come in as the seconds tick by at a glacial pace.

My phone vibrates noisily next to me and I look over, but it's just a notification from her app, telling me it's time to take my nighttime meds and set up my G-tube feeding. I look behind me at my bedside table, where I've already laid out a chocolate pudding cup and my meds, ready to be taken.

Like clockwork, my computer screen lights up, Stella's long-awaited call coming in.

I hover over the accept button, stifling my smile as I wait a few seconds to pick up, my fingers tapping away on the track-pad. I click accept and fake a big yawn when her face appears on my screen, casually glancing at my phone.

"Is it time for the nighttime meds already?"

She gives me a big smile. "Don't give me that. I see your pills behind you on your bedside table."

Embarrassed, I open my mouth to say something, but shake my head, letting her have just this one.

We take our meds together, then get our tube-feeding bags out to set up for the night. After pouring the formulas in, we hang the bags, attach the tubing, and adjust the pump rate for how long we'll be asleep. I fumble with mine, and glance over at Stella to make sure I'm doing it right. It's been a minute since I've done it myself. After that we prime the pump to get all the air out, our eyes meeting as we wait for the formula to make its way down the tube.

I start to whistle the *Jeopardy!* theme song while we wait, which makes her laugh.

"Don't look!" she says when the formula gets to the end of the tube. She lifts her shirt up just high enough to attach her G-tube.

I look away, hiding a grin, and inhale sharply, flexing the

best I can while I lift up my shirt and attach the tube to the button sticking out of my abdomen.

Glancing up, I catch her eye through the video chat.

"Take a picture, it'll last longer," I say, pulling down my shirt as she rolls her eyes. Her cheeks are just the tiniest bit red.

I sit down on my bed, pulling my laptop closer to me.

She yawns, taking her bun out, her long brown hair falling gently down, over her shoulders. I try not to stare, but she looks *good.* More like her videos. Relaxed. Happy.

"You should get some sleep," I say as she rubs her eyes sleepily. "You had a packed few days of bossing me around."

She laughs, nodding.

"Good night, Will."

"Night, Stella," I say, hesitating before pressing the end-call button and closing my laptop.

I lie back, putting my hands behind my head, the room seeming uncomfortably quiet even though it's still just me in here. But as I roll over and turn out the light, I realize for the first time in a long time, I don't really feel alone.

CHAPTER 9

STELLA

Dr. Hamid frowns as I lift up my shirt, her dark eyebrows knitting together as she looks at the infected skin around my G-tube. I wince as she gently touches the inflamed red skin, and she mumbles an apology at my reaction.

When I woke up this morning, I noticed the infection had gotten worse. When I saw the discharge oozing around the hole, I called her right away.

After a minute of inspection she finally stands, exhaling. "Let's try Bactroban and see how it looks in a day or two. Maybe we can clear it up, huh?"

I pull my shirt down, shooting her a doubtful look. I've already been at the hospital a week, and while my fever is down and my sore throat is gone, this has only gotten worse. She reaches out and gives my arm a comforting squeeze. I hope she's right, though. Because if she's not, that means surgery. And that'd be the exact opposite of *not* worrying Mom and Dad.

My phone begins to chirp away, and I look over, expecting it to be Will, but I see a message from my mom.

Cafeteria for lunch? Meet me in 15?

"Fifteen" means she's already on her way. I've been putting her off all week, telling her things are so routine, she'd be bored, but she's not taking no for an answer this time. I shoot back a yes and sigh, standing up to get changed. "Thanks, Dr. Hamid."

She smiles at me as she leaves. "Keep me updated, Stella. Barb'll keep an eye on it too."

I pull on a clean pair of leggings and a sweatshirt, make a note to add Bactroban to the schedule in my app, then head up the elevator and across into Building 2. My mom is already standing outside the cafeteria when I get there, her hair in a messy ponytail, dark circles hanging heavily under her eyes.

She looks thinner than I do.

I give her a big hug, trying not to wince when she rubs against my G-tube. "Everything okay?" she asks, her eyes appraising me.

I nod. "Great! Treatments are a breeze. Breathing better already. Everything okay with you?" I ask, studying her face.

She nods, giving me a big smile that doesn't quite reach her eyes. "Yep, everything's good!"

We get in the long line and get our usuals, a Caesar salad for her, a burger and milk shake for me, and a heaping plate of french fries for us to share.

We manage to grab a seat in the corner by the wide glass windows, a comfortable distance away from everyone else. I glance outside as we eat to see that the snow is still gently falling, a blanket of white steadily accumulating on the ground. I hope my mom leaves before it gets too bad out there.

I've finished my burger and 75 percent of the fries in the amount of time it takes my mom to eat about three bites of her salad. I watch as she picks at her food, face tired. She looks like she's been Googling again, up until the early hours of the morning, reading page after page, article after article, on lung transplants.

My dad was the only one who used to be able to keep her calm, pulling her away from her worry spiral with just a look, comforting her in a way nothing else could.

"The Divorce Diet doesn't look good on you, Mom."

She looks up at me, surprised. "What are you talking about?"

"You're too thin. Dad needs a bath. You guys are stealing my look!"

Can't you see you need each other? I want to say.

She laughs, grabbing my milk shake.

"No!" I shout as she takes a dramatic gulp. I dive across the table, trying to wrestle it back, but the lid flies off, chocolate milk shake absolutely covering the both of us. For the first time in a while, we completely crack up.

My mom takes a pile of napkins, gently wiping the shake

off my face, her eyes suddenly brimming with tears. I grab her hand, frowning.

"Mom. What?"

"I look at you and think . . . they said you wouldn't . . ." She shakes her head as she holds my face in both her hands, tears spilling out of her eyes. "But here you are. And you're grown. And beautiful. You keep proving them wrong."

She grabs a napkin, wiping away the tears. "I don't know what I'd do without you."

My insides turn cold. *I don't know what I'd do without you.*

I swallow hard and give her hand a comforting squeeze, but my mind instantly travels to the G-tube. The spreadsheets. The app. A big *35 percent* practically sitting on my chest. Until I get the transplant, that number isn't going back up. Until then, I'm the only one who can keep me alive. And I have to. I have to stay alive.

Because I'm pretty sure keeping me alive is the only thing keeping my parents going.

After my mom leaves, I head straight to the gym with Will, wanting to strengthen my weak lungs as much as I possibly can. I almost tell him not to come so I can think everything over, but I know he probably hasn't set foot in the gym in ages.

Plus, the combined worry of my parents and that thought would be too much for me to allow me to concentrate on anything else. At least Will going to the gym is a problem I can solve immediately.

I start pedaling on a stationary bike. I haven't minded my afternoon workouts ever since the gym became one of the nicest places in the entire hospital. They renovated it three years ago and practically quadrupled its size, putting in basketball courts, a saltwater pool, shiny new cardio equipment, and rows and rows of free weights. There is even an entire separate room for yoga and meditating, with wide windows looking out over the courtyard. Before that the gym here had been an old, dingy room, with a handful of mismatched dumbbells and decaying equipment that looked like it was made about a year after the wheel had been invented.

I look over to see Will holding on to a treadmill for dear life, gasping for breath as he power walks. His portable oxygen is slung over his shoulder in that classic, trendy CFer-exercising style.

I practically dragged him here, and I have to admit, it's fun for me to see him concentrating too hard to be snarky. He couldn't even use his "banned from leaving the third floor" excuse, because Barb is on the night shift today, and Julie was more than enthusiastic to have Will off doing something that will actually improve his lung function and overall health.

"So, when does this little deal of ours become mutually beneficial?" he manages to get out, looking across the entire room at me while I pedal away. He slows the speed down, gasping out words between breaths. "I've done everything you've asked with no return on my investment."

"I'm gross. Too sweaty," I say as a bead of sweat drips down my face.

He slams the stop button on the treadmill, the machine halting abruptly as he spins around to face me, fixing his nose cannula as he struggles to catch his breath. "And my hair is dirty, and I'm too tired, and my med cart is—"

"You want to draw me sweaty? Fine! I'll sweat harder!" I start to pedal like my life depends on it, my RPM quadrupling. My lungs begin to burn and I start coughing, oxygen hissing out of my cannula as I struggle for air. My legs slow down as I go into a coughing fit, before finally catching my breath.

He shakes his head. I immediately look back down at the glaring digital numbers on the bike, trying to ignore the red creeping slowly up my face.

Afterward we both exhaustedly make our way to the empty yoga room, me walking six feet ahead. I sit down against the wide windows, the glass cool from the blanket of white on the other side, covering everything in sight.

"Do I need to pose or anything?" I ask, my hand reaching up as I fix my hair. I strike a dramatic pose, which makes him laugh.

He pulls out his sketchbook and a charcoal pencil, surprising me as he puts on a pair of blue latex gloves. "Nah, just act natural."

Oh, good, yeah. That'll be easy.

I watch him, his deep-blue eyes focused on the paper, his dark eyebrows furrowing as he concentrates. He looks up, meeting my eyes as he studies me again. I look away quickly, pulling my pocket notebook out and flipping to the page for today.

"What's that?" he asks, pointing to the notebook with his pencil.

"My to-do list," I explain, crossing off number 12, "Work out," and heading to the very bottom of my list to write "Will drawing."

"A to-do list?" he asks. "Pretty old school for someone who builds apps."

"Yeah, well, the app doesn't give me the satisfaction of doing this." I take my pencil and draw a line through "Will drawing."

He fakes a sad face. "Now that really hurts my feelings."

I duck my head, but he sees the smile I'm trying to hide.

"So, what else is on the list?" he asks, looking back down at the drawing and then back up at me before starting to shade something in.

"Which list?" I ask. "My master list or my daily list?"

He laughs warmly, shaking his head. "Of course you have two lists."

"Immediate and long-term! It makes sense," I shoot back, which only makes him smirk.

"Hit me with the master list. That's the big stuff."

I flip through the pages, getting to the master list. I haven't looked at this page in a while. It's filled with different-colored inks, reds and blues and blacks, and a couple of sparkly fluorescent colors from a gel pen kit I got back in sixth grade.

"Let's see here." My finger trails up to the top. "'Volunteer for an important political cause.' Done."

I draw a line through it.

"'Study all the works of William Shakespeare.' Done!"

I draw a line through that one.

"'Share everything I know about CF with others.' I have this, uh, YouTube page. . . ."

I draw a line through it and look up at Will to see him not at all surprised. Someone's been checking up on me.

"So is your plan to die really, really smart so you can join the debate team of the dead?" He points out the window with his pencil. "You ever think about, I don't know . . . traveling the world or something?"

I look back down to see number 27, "Sistine Chapel with Abby." No line through it.

I clear my throat, moving on. "'Learn to play the piano.' Done! 'Speak fluent French'—"

Will cuts me off. "Seriously, do you ever do anything off list? No offense, but none of that sounds fun." I close the notebook, and he continues. "You want to hear my list? Take a painting class with Bob Ross. Lots of happy little trees and cadmium yellow that you don't think will work but then . . ."

"He's dead," I tell him.

He gives me a lopsided grin. "Ah, well, then I guess I'll just have to settle for sex in the Vatican!"

I roll my eyes at him. "I think you have a better shot at meeting Bob Ross."

He winks but then his face gets serious. More serious than I've ever seen it. "Okay, okay. I'd like to travel the world and really get to *see* it, you know? Not just the inside of hospitals." He looks back down and keeps sketching. "They're kind of all the same. Same generic rooms. Same tile floors. Same sterile smell. I've been everywhere without actually seeing anything."

I look at him, really look, watching the way his hair falls into his eyes when he draws, the look of concentration on his face, no more smirking expression. I wonder what it would be like to go all around the world but never be able to get outside the walls of the hospital. I don't mind being in the hospital. I feel safe here. Comfortable. But I've been coming to the same one pretty much my whole life. It's home.

If I were in Cabo this past week but stuck inside a hospital, I wouldn't just be bummed. I'd be miserable.

"Thank you," I say.

"For what?" he asks, looking up to meet my eyes.

"For saying something real."

He watches me a second before running his fingers through his hair. He's the one who's uncomfortable for a change. "Your eyes are hazel," he says, pointing at the sunlight trickling in through the glass all around me. "I didn't know that until I saw them in the sunlight. I thought they were brown."

My heart thumps loudly in my chest at his words, and the warm way he's looking at me.

"They're really nice eyes," he says a second later, a faint red creeping onto his cheeks. He looks down, scribbling away and clearing his throat. "I mean to, like, draw."

I bite on my lower lip to hide my smile.

For the first time I feel the weight of every single inch, every millimeter, of the six feet between us. I pull my sweatshirt closer to my body, looking away at the pile of yoga mats in the corner, trying to ignore the fact that that open space? It will always be there.

That evening I scroll through Facebook for the first time all day, looking at all the pictures my friends are posting from Cabo. I throw a heart onto Camila's new profile picture. She's standing on a surfboard in her striped bikini, a big goofy smile on her face, her shoulders burnt to a crisp, all my SPF warnings utterly ignored. But Mya sent me a behind-the-scenes Snap video earlier this afternoon, taken seconds after this picture, which revealed that Camila still has no clue how to surf. She maybe balanced for about three and a half seconds, shooting the camera a big smile before flailing off the surfboard a second later.

I do a little victory dance when I scroll to a picture Mason posted, his tan arm slung around Mya's shoulder. I almost fall out of my chair when I see the caption. "Cabo Cutie." Grinning, I give it a quick like before closing the app to send her a text.

Way to go, Mya!!! With heart eye emojis for days.

I glance over to see my pocket notebook still open to my master list. My eyes are pulled back to number 27, "Sistine Chapel with Abby." I open my laptop and my mouse hovers over a blue folder labeled "Abs."

I hesitate for a second before clicking on it, a sea of pictures and videos and artwork from my sister filling my screen. I click on a GoPro video she sent me two years ago, her balancing on top of a high, rickety bridge. The screen is filled with the dizzying image of the distance from where she's sitting to the river below, the water underneath her strong enough to overtake anything in its path.

"Pretty crazy, huh, Stella?" she says as the camera swings back to her and she adjusts her harness one more time. "I thought you might like to see how this feels!"

She clicks her helmet in place, the GoPro view shifting back to show the edge of the bridge and the long, long way down. "And I brought my jumping buddy!" She holds up my stuffed panda, the one right next to me now, giving him a big squeeze.

"I'll hold him tight, don't worry!" Then, without even

a second thought, she launches herself off the bridge. I fly through the air with her, her delighted whoops echoing loudly through the speakers.

Then comes the bounce. We fly back up, the panda's face coming onto the screen, Abby's voice, breathless and giddy as she grips the panda tightly, screaming out, "Happy birthday, Stella!"

Swallowing hard, I slam the laptop shut, knocking over a can of soda on the side table. The bubbling cola spills out all over the table and the floor. Great.

I reach down to pick up the can, hopping over the puddle, and toss it into the trash bin on my way out into the hall. As I walk around the nurses' station, I notice Barb dozing off in a chair, her head lolling to one side, her mouth slightly open. Carefully, I open the door to the janitor's closet, grabbing the paper towels from a packed shelf of cleaning supplies and trying not to wake her.

She hears me, though, and looks up, her eyes sleepy.

"You work too hard," I say when she sees me.

She smiles and opens her arms like she used to when I was younger and having a rough day at the hospital.

I climb onto her lap, like a child, and wrap my arms around her neck, smelling the familiar, safe, vanilla scent of her perfume. Resting my head on her shoulder, I close my eyes and pretend.

CHAPTER 10

WILL

"Cevaflomalin time!" Julie sings, swinging my door open the next morning, a bag of the medicine in her hand.

I nod. I already got the notification from Stella's app and moved from the desk over to my bed, where the IV rack is, waiting for her arrival.

I watch as Julie hangs the bag, taking the IV line and turning toward me. Her eyes travel to the drawing I did of Stella in the yoga room, hanging next to the lung drawing Stella had put up above my desk, the corner of her lip turning up as she looks at it.

"I like seeing you like this," she says, her eyes meeting mine.

"Like how?" I ask, pulling down the neck of my shirt.

She inserts the IV line into a port on my chest. "Hopeful."

I think about Stella, my eyes traveling to the IV bag of Cevaflomalin. I reach out to touch it gently, feeling the weight of the bag in my palm. The trial is so new. Still too new to know how this will turn out.

It's the first time I've even let myself think about it . . . which might be dangerous. Or even stupid.

I don't know. Getting my hopes up when a hospital is involved doesn't seem like a good idea to me.

"What if this doesn't work?" I ask.

I don't *feel* any different. Not yet, at least.

I watch the IV bag, the steady drip, drip, drip of the medicine working its way into my body. I look back at Julie, the both of us silent for a moment.

"But what if it does?" she asks, touching my shoulder. I watch her leave.

But what if it does.

After the IV drip, I carefully slide on a pair of bright-blue gloves, making sure to keep my B. cepacia germs far away from anything Stella will touch.

I take one more look at my drawing from the yoga room earlier, carefully evaluating it as I pull it down off the wall.

It's a cartoon but it's definitely Stella. She's in a white doctor's coat, a stethoscope slung around her neck, her small cartoon hands resting angrily on her hips. Squinting at the drawing, I realize it's missing something.

Aha.

I grab red, orange, and yellow pencils and draw fire coming

out of her mouth. *Way* more realistic. Laughing to myself, I take a manila envelope that I stole from the nurses' station, slide the drawing inside, and scrawl on the outside: "Inside, you'll find my heart and soul. Be kind."

I walk down the hall to her room, picturing her opening the envelope, expecting something profound and deep. I look both ways before slipping it under the door, and lean against the wall, listening.

I hear her soft footsteps on the other side of the door, the sound of her snapping gloves on, then bending over to grab the envelope. There's silence. More silence. And finally—a laugh! A real, genuine, warm laugh.

Victory! I walk back down the hallway, whistling, sliding onto my bed and grabbing my phone as FaceTime pings, a call coming in from Stella just like I hoped.

I answer it, her face appearing, her pink lips turning up at the corners. "A dragon lady? So sexist!"

"Hey, you're lucky you said no nudes!"

She laughs again, looking at the drawing and then back at me. "Why cartoons?"

"They're subversive, you know? They can look light and fun on the outside, but they have punch." I could talk about this all day. If there's anything I'm passionate about, this would be it. I hold up a book that's on my nightstand that has some of the best of the *New York Times* political cartoons. "Politics, religion, society. I think a well-drawn cartoon can say more than words ever could, you know? It could change *minds*."

She looks at me, surprised, not saying anything.

I shrug, realizing how hard I just nerded out. "I mean, I'm just a wannabe cartoonist. What do I know."

I point at the drawing behind her, a beautiful picture of lungs, flowers pouring out of the inside, a backdrop of stars behind them. "Now *that* is art." I pull my laptop closer to me, realizing what it means. "Healthy lungs! That's brilliant. Who did it?"

She looks back at it, pausing. "My older sister. Abby."

"That's some talent. I'd love to take a look at her other work!"

A strange look comes onto her face, and her voice turns cold. "Look. We're not friends. We're not sharing our stories. This is just about doing our treatments, okay?"

The call ends abruptly, my own confused face swinging into view. What the hell was that? I jump up, angry, and throw open the door to my room. Storming down the hallway, I make a beeline for her door, ready to give her a piece of my mind. She can kiss my—

"Hey! Will!" a voice says behind me.

I swing around, surprised to see Hope and Jason walking toward me. I was texting Jason like an hour ago, and I still totally forgot they were coming today, like they always do on Fridays. Jason holds up a bag of food, grinning at me as the smell of fries from my favorite diner a block away from our school wafts down the hallway, trying to reel me in.

I freeze, looking between Stella's door and my visitors.

And that's when it hits me.

I've seen both of her parents come and go. I saw her friends visiting her the first day she got here.

But Abby? She hasn't even *talked* about Abby.

Where has Abby been?

I walk up to Hope and Jason, grabbing the bag and nodding for them to follow me into my room. "Come with me!"

I throw open my laptop, the two of them standing behind me as it boots up, surprised expressions on their faces.

"Nice to see you, too, dude," Jason says, peering over my shoulder.

"So, I met a girl," I say, facing the both of them. I shake my head when Hope gives me one of *those* smiles, her eyes excited. Jason is completely up to date on all things Stella, but I haven't filled Hope in yet. Mostly because I knew she'd react like this. "Not like that! Okay. Maybe like that. But it can't be like that. Whatever."

I swing back to my computer, opening the tab to Stella's YouTube page and scrolling to a video from last year labeled "Polypectomy Party!" I click on it, before slamming my space bar to pause the video and spinning around to fill them in.

"She's got CF. And she's, like, a crazy control freak. She's made me start doing my treatments all the way and everything."

Relief fills Hope's eyes and Jason is positively beaming. "You've started doing your treatments again? Will. That's awesome," Hope gushes.

I wave her praise away, even though I'm a little surprised it got this big of a reaction. Hope pestered me about it for a while, but when I told them to leave it alone, they didn't make a big deal about it. I sort of thought we were all on the same page.

But now they both look so relieved. I frown. I don't want to get their hopes up.

"Yeah, yeah. Anyway. Get this. She has a sister named Abby." I fast-forward to a few minutes in, pressing play so they both can watch.

Stella and Abby are sitting in a hospital room, artwork lining the walls like in her room now. Dr. Hamid is there, a stethoscope pressed to Stella's chest as she listens to her lungs. Stella's legs are shaking anxiously as she looks between Dr. Hamid and the camera.

"Okay. So, I'm having a nasal poly . . . ?"

"Polypectomy," Dr. Hamid says, straightening up. "We're removing polyps from your nasal passages."

Stella grins at the camera. "I'm trying to talk the doc into a nose job while she's there."

Abby gives her a big hug, squeezing her tightly. "Stella's nervous. But I'll be there to sing her to sleep, just like always!" She starts to sing, her voice soft and sweet, "'I love you, a bushel and a peck—'"

"Stop!" Stella says, clamping her hand down over her sister's mouth. "You'll jinx it!"

I hit pause on the video, swinging around to face my friends.

They both look confused, clearly not getting the realization that just came to me. They look at each other, eyebrows raised, and then Hope gives me a big smile, leaning over to squint at the sidebar.

"You watched all her videos?"

I ignore her.

"Well, she just freaked out like five minutes ago when I asked to see more of her sister's art. That video was last year," I say as an explanation.

"Okay, and?" Jason asks, frowning.

"Abby's not in any of the videos after this."

They nod, slowly catching on. Hope pulls out her phone, frowning as she taps away. "I found Abby Grant's Instagram. It's mostly art, and her and Stella." She looks up at me, nodding. "But you're right. She hasn't posted in a year."

I look from Jason to Hope, then back again. "I think something happened to Abby."

The next afternoon my phone buzzes noisily, reminding me of an exercise session Stella programmed into my regimen. I haven't seen her since I figured out something happened with

Abby, and the thought of seeing her in just a few minutes is making me weirdly nervous. I couldn't really enjoy the rest of the visit with Hope and Jason, even as we ate fries and talked about all the latest post-Thanksgiving school drama over the new episode of *Westworld*. We always wait to watch new episodes together, even if I'm on an entirely different continent in another time zone and need to Skype them.

Taking a deep breath, I head to the gym to meet Stella, pushing open the door and walking past the rows of treadmills and ellipticals and stationary bikes.

Peeking into the yoga room, I see her sitting on a green mat meditating, her legs crossed, her eyes closed.

Slowly I push open the door, walking as quietly as I can to a mat across the room from her.

Six feet away.

I sit down and watch how peaceful she looks, her face soft and calm. But her eyes slowly open to meet mine and she stiffens.

"Barb didn't see you, did she?"

"Abby's dead, isn't she?" I blurt out, cutting right to the point. She stares at me, not saying anything.

Finally she swallows, shaking her head. "Real nice, Will. About as delicate as a jackhammer."

"Who has time for delicacy, Stella? We clearly don't—"

"Stop!" she says, cutting me off. "Stop reminding me that I'm dying. I know. I *know* that I'm dying."

She shakes her head, her face serious. "But I can't, Will. Not now. I have to make it."

I'm confused. "I don't under—"

"I've been dying my whole life. Every birthday, we celebrated like it was my last one." She shakes her head, her hazel eyes shining bright with tears. "But then *Abby* died. It was supposed to be me, Will. Everyone was ready for that."

She takes a deep breath, the weight of the world on her shoulders. "It will kill my parents if I die too."

It hits me like a ton of bricks. I've been wrong all along.

"The regimen. All this time I thought you were afraid of death, but it's not that at all." I watch her face as I keep talking. "You're a dying girl with survivor's guilt. That is a complete mind-fuck. How do you live with—"

"*Living* is the only choice I have, Will!" she snaps, standing up and glaring down at me.

I stand up, staring at her. Wanting to step closer and close the gap between us. Wanting to shake her to get her to see. "But, Stella. That's not living."

She turns, pulling on her face mask and bolting for the door.

"Stella, wait! Come on!" I take a few steps after her, wishing I could just reach out and grab her hand, so I can fix it. "Don't go. We're supposed to be exercising, right? I'll shut up, okay?"

The door slams behind her. Shit. I really screwed that up.

I turn my head to stare at the mat where she was just sitting, frowning at the empty space where she just was.

And I realize I'm doing the one thing I've told myself this whole time I wouldn't do. I'm wanting something I can never have.

CHAPTER 11

STELLA

I slam open the door to my room, Abby's drawings all blurring together in front of me as all the pain and the guilt I've been pushing further and further down rears its ugly head, making my knees buckle under me. I crumple onto the ground, my fingers clutching at the cold linoleum floor as I hear my mom's scream ringing in my head just like it did that morning.

I was supposed to be with her that weekend in Arizona, but I was struggling so hard to breathe the night before our flight that I had to stay behind. I apologized over and over again. It was supposed to be her birthday gift. Our first trip, just the two of us. But Abby waved it off, hugging me tight and telling me that she'd be back in a few days with enough pictures and stories to make me feel like I'd been there with her all along.

But she never came back.

I remember hearing the phone ring downstairs. My mom

sobbing, my dad knocking on my door and telling me to sit down. Something had happened.

I didn't believe him.

I shook my head, and laughed. This was an Abby prank. It had to be. It wasn't possible. It couldn't be possible. I was the one who was supposed to die, long before all of them. Abby was practically the definition of *alive.*

It took three full days for the grief to hit me. It was only when our flight back was supposed to land that I realized Abby really wasn't coming home. Then I was blindsided. I lay in bed for two weeks straight, ignoring my AffloVest and my regimen, and when I got up, it wasn't just my lungs that were a mess. My parents couldn't talk to each other. Couldn't even look at each other.

I'd seen it coming long before it happened. I'd prepared Abby for what to do to keep them together after I was gone. But I hadn't expected to be the one doing it.

I tried so hard. I planned family outings; I made dinner for them when they couldn't do anything but stare off into space. But it was all for nothing. If Abby came up, a fight always followed. If she didn't, her presence suffocated the silence. They were separated after three months. Divorced in six. Putting as much distance between each other as possible, leaving me straddling the in-between.

But it hasn't helped. Ever since then it's like I've been living a dream, every day focused on keeping myself alive to keep them both afloat. I make to-do lists and check them off, trying to keep myself busy, swallowing my grief and pain so my parents don't get consumed by theirs.

Now on top of all that, *Will*, of all people, is trying to tell me what I should be doing. As if he has any concept of what living actually means.

And the worst part is that the only person I want to talk to about it is Abby.

I angrily wipe away my tears with the back of my hand, pulling my phone out of my pocket and texting the only other person I know who will understand.

Multipurpose lounge. Now.

I think of all the drawings around my room. Each one a separate trip to the hospital with Abby there to hold my hand. And now there are three trips. Three whole trips without a drawing to go with them.

I remember the first day I came to Saint Grace's. If I hadn't been afraid before, the size of this place was enough to make a six-year-old feel overwhelmed. The big windows, the machinery, the loud noises. I walked through the lobby, clutching Abby's hand for dear life and trying so hard to be brave.

My parents talked to Barb and Dr. Hamid. Even before they knew me, they did their very best to help me feel like Saint Grace's Hospital was my second home from the moment I got there.

But, of everyone, it was Abby who really did that. She gave me three invaluable gifts that day.

The first was my stuffed panda bear, Patches, carefully hand-selected from the hospital gift shop.

The second was my first of many drawings, the tornado of stars. The first piece of "wallpaper" I'd collect from her.

And while my parents talked to Barb about the state-of-the-art facility, Abby ran off and found me the final gift of that day.

The best I'd ever receive in all my years at Saint Grace's.

"It's impressive, for sure," my mom said, while I watched Abby trot away down the brightly colored hallway of the children's ward, disappearing around a corner.

"Stella's going to be right at home here!" Barb said, giving me a warm smile. I remember clutching Patches, trying to find the courage to smile back at her.

Abby rounded the corner, nearly running smack into a nurse as she sprinted back over to us, a very small, very thin, brown-haired boy wearing an oversize Colombian national team jersey trailing behind her.

"Look! There are other kids here!"

I waved at the boy before Barb stepped in between us, colorful scrubs putting up a wall between the two of us.

"Poe, you know better," she said, scolding the small boy as Abby took my hand in hers.

But Abby had already set it in motion. Even from six feet

away Poe became my best friend. Which is why he's the only person to talk me through this.

I pace back and forth, the lounge a blur in front of me. I try to focus on the fish tank or the TV or the refrigerator humming in the corner, but I'm still livid over my fight with Will.

"You knew he had boundary issues," Poe says from behind me, watching me intently from the edge of the love seat. "For what it's worth, I don't think he meant to hurt you."

I spin around to face him, clutching at the counter of the kitchenette. "When he said 'Abby' and 'dead,'"—my voice cracks, and I dig my fingers into the cool marble of the counter—"like it was no big deal, I just . . ."

Poe shakes his head, his eyes sad.

"I should have been with her, Poe," I choke out, wiping my eyes with the back of my hand. She was always there. To stand by me when I needed her. And I wasn't there when she needed me most.

"Don't. Not again. It's not your fault. She'd tell you it's not your fault."

"Was she in pain? What if she was scared?" I gasp, the air catching in my chest. I keep seeing my sister plummeting down, like she did in the GoPro video and a million times before, bungee jumping and cliff diving with reckless abandon.

Only, this time there's no wild whoop of joy and excitement. She hits the water and doesn't resurface.

She wasn't supposed to die.

She was supposed to be the one to *live.*

"Hey! Stop. Look at me."

I stare at him, tears pouring from my eyes.

"You have to stop," he says, his fingers clutching the armrest of the couch, his knuckles turning white. "You can't know. You just . . . can't. You'll drive yourself crazy."

I take a deep breath, shaking my head. He stands up, stepping toward me and groaning in frustration. "This disease is a fucking prison! I want to hug you."

I sniff, nodding in agreement.

"Pretend I did, okay?" he says. I see he's blinking back tears too. "And know that I love you. More than food! More than the Colombian national team!"

I crack a smile, nodding. "I love you, too, Poe." He pretends to blow me a kiss, without actually breathing my way.

I slump down onto the mint-green love seat sitting vacant across from Poe's, immediately gasping in pain as my vision doubles. I sit bolt upright and clutch at my side, my G-tube burning like absolute fire.

Poe's face turns white. "Stella! Is everything okay?"

"My G-tube," I say, the pain subsiding. I sit up, shaking my head and gasping for breath. "I'm fine. I'm fine."

I take a deep breath and lift my shirt and see that the infection has only gotten way worse, the skin red and puffy, the G-tube and the area around it oozing. My eyes widen in surprise. It's only been eight days here. How have I not noticed how bad it's gotten?

Poe winces, shaking his head. "Let's get you back to your room. *Now.*"

Fifteen minutes later Dr. Hamid gently touches the infected skin around my G-tube, and I grimace as pain radiates across my stomach and chest. She takes her hand away, shaking her head as she pulls her gloves off and carefully puts them in a trash can by the door.

"We need to take care of this. It's too far gone. We have to excoriate the skin and replace your G-tube to purge the infection."

I immediately feel woozy, my insides turning cold. It's the words I've been afraid of since it first started looking infected. I put my shirt back down, trying not to let the fabric rub against the area.

"But—"

She cuts me off. "No buts. It has to be done. We are risking sepsis here. If this gets any worse, the infection can get into your bloodstream."

We're both silent, knowing how big the risk is here. If I get sepsis, I'll definitely die. But if I get put under for surgery, my lungs might not be strong enough to pull me through to the other side.

She sits down next to me, bumping my shoulder and smiling at me. "It'll be okay."

"You don't know that," I say, swallowing nervously.

She nods, her face thoughtful. "You're right. I don't." She takes a deep breath, meeting my anxious gaze. "It's risky. I won't say it's not. But sepsis is a far bigger and far more likely monster."

Fear creeps up my neck and wraps itself around my entire body. But she's right.

Dr. Hamid picks up the panda sitting next to me, looking at it and smiling faintly. "You're a fighter, Stella. You always have been."

Holding out the bear to me, she looks into my eyes. "Tomorrow morning, then?"

I reach out, taking the panda, nodding. "Tomorrow morning."

"I'm going to call your parents and let them know," she says, and I freeze, a wave of dread hitting me.

"Can you give it a few minutes so I can break the news to them? It'll be easier coming from me."

She nods, giving my shoulder a tight squeeze before leaving. I lie back, clinging to Patches, anxiety filling me as I think about the calls I have to make. I keep hearing my mom in the cafeteria, her voice weaving circles around my head.

I don't know what I'd do without you.

I don't know what I'd do without you.

I don't know what I'd do without you.

I hear a noise outside my door and turn my head to see

an envelope sliding underneath. I watch the light trickling in from under the door as a pair of feet stand there for a moment before slowly turning and walking away.

I stand carefully and bend down to pick up the envelope. Opening it, I pull out a cartoon drawing, the colors sad and dull. It's a picture of a frowning Will, a wilted bouquet of flowers in his hand, a bubble caption underneath it reading "Sorry."

I lie back down on my bed, holding the drawing to my chest and closing my eyes tightly.

Dr. Hamid said I was a fighter.

But I really don't know that I am anymore.

CHAPTER 12

WILL

I messed up bad. I know that.

I sneak out of our wing and around the east lobby of the hospital after dropping off the drawing, my phone clutched in my hand as I wait for *something*. A text, a FaceTime call, *anything*.

She must have seen the drawing by now, right? Her light was on. But it's been radio silence since our fight.

What should I do? She won't even talk to me, I text Jason, grimacing at myself. I can see him getting a real kick over me hung up on someone enough to ask his advice.

Just give her some time, man, he replies.

I sigh loudly, frustrated. Time. All this waiting is agony.

I plop down on a bench, watching people pass by as they go through the sliding doors of the hospital. Young kids, nervously clutching the hands of their parents. Nurses, rubbing their eyes sleepily as they finally get to leave. Visitors, eagerly pulling on their jackets as they head home for the night. For the first time in a few days I wish I were one of them.

My stomach growls noisily and I decide to head to the cafeteria to distract myself with some food. Walking toward the elevator, I freeze when I hear a familiar voice pouring out of a room nearby.

"*No envíe dinero, no puede pagarlo,*" the voice says, the tone somber, sad. *Dinero.* Money. I took two years of Spanish in high school and can say only a handful of phrases, but I recognize that word. I peek my head inside to see it's a chapel, with big stained-glass windows and classic wooden pews. The old, churchy look is so different from the rest of the hospital's modern, sleek design.

My eyes land on Poe, sitting in the front row, his elbows resting on his knees as he talks to someone over FaceTime.

"*Yo también te extraño,*" he says. "*Lo sé. Te amo, Mamá.*"

He hangs up the phone, putting his head in his hands. I pull the heavy door open a bit wider, the hinges creaking loudly as I do.

He turns around in surprise.

"The chapel?" I ask, my voice echoing too loud off the walls of the wide space as I make my way down the aisle toward him.

He looks around, smiling faintly. "My mom likes to see me in here. I'm Catholic, but she's *Catholic.*"

He sighs, leaning his head against the pew. "I haven't seen her in two years. She wants me to come visit her."

My eyes widen in surprise and I sit down across the aisle, a safe distance away. That's a really long time. "You haven't seen your mom in two years? What did she do to you?"

He shakes his head, his dark eyes filled with sadness. "It's not like that. They got deported back to Colombia. But I was born here and they didn't want to take me away from my doctors. I'm a 'ward of the state' until I'm eighteen."

Shit. I can't even imagine what that was like. How could they deport the parents of someone with CF? The parents of someone *terminal.*

"That's fucked up," I say.

Poe nods. "I miss them. So much."

I frown, running my fingers through my hair. "Poe, you have to go! You have to visit them."

He sighs, fixing his eyes on the large wooden cross sitting behind the pulpit, and I remember what I overheard. *Dinero.* "It's pricey. She wants to send money, but she can't really afford it. And I'm certainly not going to take food off her table—"

"Listen, if it's money, I can help. Seriously. I'm not trying to be a privileged dick, but it's not an issue—" But before I even finish, I know it's a no go.

"Come on. Stop." He turns his head to give me a look, before his face softens. "I'll . . . I'll figure it out."

A silence falls over us, the quiet, open air of the big room making my ears ring. This isn't just about money. Besides, I know more than anyone that money can't fix everything. Maybe someday my mom will catch on.

"Thanks, though," Poe says finally, smiling at me. "I mean it."

I nod as we fall silent again. How is it fair that my mom can hover over me, while someone else has his just ripped away from him? Here I am, counting down to eighteen, while Poe is trying to slow time down, wishing for more of it.

More time.

For me, it was easy to give up. It was easy to fight my treatments and focus on the time I do have. Stop working so damn hard for just a few seconds more. But Stella and Poe are making me want every second more that I can get.

And that terrifies me more than anything else.

That evening I lie on my bed, staring up at the ceiling as I do my nebulizer treatment without Stella.

Anything? Jason texts me, which doesn't help, since the answer is a resounding no.

Still nothing from her. Not even a note. But I can't stop thinking about her. And the longer she's silent, the worse it gets. I can't stop thinking about what it would be like to be close to her, to reach out and actually *touch* her, to make her feel better after I screwed up.

I can feel something reaching from deep in my chest, in the tips of my fingers and the pit of my stomach. Reaching out to feel the smooth skin of her arm, the raised scars I'm sure are on her body.

But I'll never be able to. The distance between us will never go away or change.

Six feet forever.

My phone pings and I grab it, hopeful, but it's just a notification from Twitter. I throw my phone down on my bed, frustrated.

What the hell, Stella? She can't stay mad forever.

Can she?

I need to make this right.

I switch off the nebulizer and throw my legs over the bed, sliding into my shoes and peering into the hallway to make sure the coast is clear. I see Julie sliding into a room farther down the hall with an IV drip, and I quickly slip out of my room, knowing I have time. Walking quietly down the hallway, I pass the empty nurses' station and freeze in front of her door, hearing music softly playing on the other side.

She's in there.

Taking a deep breath, I knock, the sound of my knuckles reverberating off the worn wood.

I hear the music shut off and then her footsteps as she comes closer and closer, stopping in front of the door, hesitating.

Finally it opens, her hazel eyes making my heart pound heavily in my chest.

It's so good to see her.

"You're here," I say softly.

"I'm here," she says coolly, leaning against the doorframe and acting like she didn't just ignore me for the whole day. "I got your cartoon. You're forgiven. Back up."

I quickly step all the way back to the far wall, putting the six frustrating feet between us. We stare at each other, and she blinks, looking away to check the hall for nurses before looking down at the tile floor.

"You missed our treatment."

She looks impressed that I actually remembered but stays silent. I notice her eyes are red, like she's been crying. And I don't think it's from what I said.

"What's going on?"

She takes a deep breath, and when she speaks, I can hear the nerves lacing her words. "The skin around my G-tube is pretty badly infected. Dr. Hamid's worried about sepsis. She's going to purge my infected skin and replace my G-tube in the morning."

When I look in her eyes, I see it's way more than nerves. She's afraid. I want to reach out and take her hand in mine. I want to tell her that everything will be okay and that this shouldn't be a bad one.

"I'm going under general."

What? General anesthesia? With her lungs at 35 percent? Is Dr. Hamid out of her mind?

I grip the railing on the wall to keep myself in place. "Shit. Are your lungs up for that?" We stare at each other for a moment, the open air between us feeling like miles and miles.

She looks away, ignoring the question. "Remember to take your bedtime meds and then set up your G-tube feeding for the night, okay?" Without giving me time to respond, she closes the door.

I walk slowly to it, reaching out to lay my hand flat against it, knowing she's on the other side. I take a deep breath, resting my head on the door, my voice barely a whisper. "It's going to be okay, Stella."

My fingers land on a sign hanging on her door. I look up, reading it: NOTHING TO EAT OR DRINK AFTER MIDNIGHT. SURGERY 6 A.M.

I pull my hand away before I get busted by one of the nurses and walk down the hallway to my room, plopping down on my bed. Stella is normally so in control. Why is this time so different? Is it because of her parents? Because of how low her lung function is?

I roll over on my side, my eyes landing on my own lung drawing, making me remember the drawing in her room.

Abby.

Of course that's why she's so freaked out. This is her first surgery without Abby.

I still need to make things right. An idea pops into my head and I sit bolt upright. Grabbing my phone from my pocket, I set an alarm for 5:00 a.m., for the first time maybe ever. Then I take my box of art supplies off my shelf and get planning.

CHAPTER 13

STELLA

I hold Patches close to my chest and look from my mom to my dad as they sit on either side of me. Both of them shoot me thin-lipped smiles that don't reach their eyes as they avoid each other's gazes. I look over at the picture of all of us pinned to the back of my door, wishing I could have those parents back, the ones who always told me everything would be okay.

Taking a deep breath, I suppress a cough, while my dad tries to make some small talk.

He holds up the pink calendar they sent around to all the rooms with the daily specials down at the cafeteria. "I think there's gonna be cream of broccoli soup tonight for dinner. Your favorite, Stell!"

"She probably won't be up for eating right after surgery, Tom," my mom snaps at him, his face falling at her words.

I try to sound enthusiastic. "If I'm up for it tonight, I'll definitely get some!"

There's a knock on the door and an orderly walks in, wearing a surgical cap and a pair of blue latex gloves. My parents both stand up, my dad reaching out to take my hand.

It takes everything in me to steady it.

"See you in a few, honey," my mom says as both of them give me big hugs, which linger a little too long. I wince as my G-tube rubs up against them, but I hold on tight, not wanting them to let go.

The orderly pulls up the railings on the sides of my gurney, locking them in place with a click. I stare at Abby's drawing as they roll me out, the healthy lungs calling to me. I wish more than anything she were here with me now, holding my hand, singing the song.

The orderly rolls me down the hallway, my parents' faces fading as they get farther and farther away, and we get into the elevator at the end of the hall. As the doors slide shut, the orderly smiles at me. I try to smile back, but my mouth refuses to make the shape. I clutch at the sheets, my fingers interlacing with the fabric.

The door dings open, the familiar hallways whizz by, everything seeming too bright, too whitewashed to make out specifics.

We go through the heavy double doors into the pre-op area, and then into a room slightly down the hallway. The orderly pushes the gurney into place. "Need anything before I head out?" he asks.

I shake my head, trying to take a deep breath as he leaves, the room becoming completely silent except for the steady beeping of my monitors.

I stare at the ceiling, trying to push away the growing panic eating away at my insides. I did everything right. I was careful and put on the Fucidin, I took my medication at the scheduled times, and I'm still lying here about to go into surgery anyway.

All of my obsessing over my regimen for nothing.

I think I get it now. Why Will would go onto the roof. I'd do anything to get up from the gurney and run far, far away. To Cabo. To Vatican City to see the Sistine Chapel. To all the things I have avoided out of fear of getting sicker, only to find myself lying here anyway, about to go into another surgery I might not come out of.

My fingers wrap around the railings clicked into place on either side of me, my knuckles turning white as I tighten my grip on them, willing myself to be a fighter like Dr. Hamid said yesterday. If I want to do those things, I need more time. I have to fight for it.

The door slowly opens, and a tall, thin person ducks inside. He's wearing the same green surgeon scrubs, face mask, and blue gloves that the pre-op nurses wear, but his wavy brown hair is peeking out from under a clear surgical cap.

His eyes find mine and I let go of the railings in surprise.

"What are you doing here?" I whisper, watching as Will

sits down in a chair beside me, scooting it back to make sure he's a safe distance away.

"It's your first surgery without Abby," he says in explanation, a new expression I don't quite recognize filling his blue eyes. It's not mocking or jokey, it's totally and completely open. Almost earnest.

I swallow hard, trying to stop the emotions that come bubbling up, tears clouding my eyes. "How did you know that?"

"I've seen all your movies," he says, his eyes crinkling at the corners as he smiles at me. "You might say I'm a fan."

All of them? Even that embarrassing one from when I was twelve?

"I might mess this up," he says, clearing his throat as he pulls a sheet of paper from his pocket.

He starts to sing, softly.

"I love you, a bushel and a peck—"

"Go away. I'm being stupid," I blubber as I wipe the tears away with the back of my hand, shaking my head.

"A bushel and a peck and a hug around the neck."

Abby's song. He's singing Abby's song. The tears start rolling down my face faster than I can catch them as I watch his deep-blue eyes, focused on reading every lyric off that crumpled piece of paper.

I feel like my heart might burst, I'm feeling so many things at once. "My gran used to sing us that song. I never loved it, but Abby did."

He laughs, shaking his head. "I had to Google it. Man, it is *old*."

I laugh with him, nodding. "I know. What the hell is a—"

"Barrel and a heap?" we say at the same time, the both of us laughing, his eyes meeting mine and making my heart dance inside my chest, the heart monitor just next to him beeping faster and faster. He leans forward, ever so slightly, just barely in the danger zone, but enough to push away the pain of the G-tube.

"You're going to be just fine, Stella."

His voice is deep. Soft. I know in that moment, even though it could not be more ridiculous, that if I die in there, I won't die without falling in love.

"Promise?" I ask.

He nods and stretches his arm out, holding up a gloved pinky across the distance. I take it and we pinky promise. The smallest contact, but the first time we've ever touched.

And right now that doesn't scare me.

My head snaps in the direction of the door as the sound of footsteps comes closer and closer. Dr. Hamid appears, a surgical nurse pushing through the door with her.

"Ready to get this show on the road?" she says, shooting me a thumbs-up.

My head whips around to the chair where Will was sitting, fear gripping my chest.

It's empty.

And then I see him, behind the gray curtain, his back

pressed up against the wall. He holds his finger to his mouth and pulls his face mask off to smile at me.

I smile back, and as I look at him, I start to believe what he said.

I'm going to be fine.

A few minutes later I'm lying on the operating table, the room dim except for the blinding light directly above my head.

"All right, Stella, you know what to do," a voice says, holding up a mask in a blue-gloved hand.

My heart begins pounding nervously, and I turn my head to face them, meeting their dark eyes as they put the mask over my nose and mouth. When I wake up, it will all be over.

"Ten," I say, looking past the anesthesiologist to the operating room wall, my eyes landing on a shape that's oddly familiar.

Abby's lung drawing.

How?

But I know of course. Will. He snuck it into the operating room. A single tear falls from my eye and I keep counting.

"Nine. Eight." The flowers all start to swim together, the blues and the pinks and the whites all twisting and turning and blurring together, the colors coming off the page and reaching toward me.

"Seven. Six. Five." The night sky suddenly comes to life, swimming past the flowers, the stars filling the air around me.

They twinkle and dance above my head, close enough for me to reach out and touch them.

I hear a voice humming, somewhere in the distance. "A Bushel and a Peck."

"Four. Three."

The edges of my vision start going black, my world going darker and darker. I focus on a single star, a single point of light, getting brighter and warmer and more overwhelming.

The humming stops and I hear a voice, far-off and muddled. Abby. Oh my god. It's Abby's voice.

". . . back . . . don't."

"Two," I whisper, not sure if it's in my head or out loud. And then I see her. I see Abby, right there in front of me, blurry at first and then as clear as day. My dad's curly hair, and her larger-than-life smile, and her hazel eyes identical to my own.

". . . more . . . time . . ."

She's pushing me away from the light.

"One."

Darkness.

CHAPTER 14

WILL

I quietly push open the door, looking both ways before sneaking out of the pre-op area and almost running smack into a nurse. I quickly look away and put my face mask up to disguise myself as she heads inside.

I take a few quick steps and hide behind the wall next to the stairwell, noticing a man and a woman sitting on opposite sides of the empty waiting room.

Squinting, I look from one to the other.

I know them from somewhere.

"Can I ask you a question?" the man says, and the woman looks up to meet his eyes, her jaw tightening.

She looks like an older Stella. The same full lips, the same thick eyebrows, the same expressive eyes.

Stella's parents.

She nods just once, looking wary. You can practically cut the tension with a knife. I know I should leave. I know I should open the stairwell door and get back before I get in trouble, but something makes me stay.

"The tile in my bathroom is, uh, purple? What color bath mat do I—"

"Black," she says, putting her head back down and looking at her hands, her hair falling in front of her face.

There's a moment of silence and I see the door into the hallway quietly open, Barb sliding through. Neither of them notices her come in. Stella's dad clears his throat. "And the towels?"

She throws up her hands, exasperated. "It doesn't matter, Tom."

"It mattered when we painted the office. You said the rug—"

"Our daughter's in surgery and you want to talk about *towels*?" she snaps, her face livid. I've never seen Barb look so displeased. She crosses her arms, standing up a little straighter as she watches their back-and-forth.

"I just wanna talk," her dad says softly. "About anything."

"Oh my god. You're killing me. Stop. . . ." Her voice trails off as they both look over to see Barb, her face steadily growing angrier and angrier until it has the same look that she gives us when we get in trouble.

She takes a deep breath, pulling all the air from the room. "I can't *imagine* what you've been through, losing Abby," she says, her voice deathly serious. "But *Stella*"—she points at the pre-op doors, where somewhere in the distance, Stella is lying on a table about to be operated on—"Stella is fighting for her life in there. And she's doing it for *you.*"

They both look away, ashamed.

"You can't be friends? At least be adults," Barb fires at them, her voice filled with frustration.

Dang, Barb. Take it to *church.*

Stella's mom shakes her head. "I can't be around him. I look at his face and I see Abby."

Her dad looks up quickly, barely taking in her face before he looks away again. "I see Stella when I look at you."

"You *are* their parents. Did you forget that part of the deal? Did you know that when she found out about the surgery, she insisted on telling you herself because she was so afraid of how you'd take it?" Barb says, looking up.

God, no wonder Stella was so obsessive about staying alive. These people lost their child and then they lost each other. If she died, they'd probably lose their minds.

My dad left before I got sicker and sicker, before the CF could take a toll on my body. He couldn't handle a sick child. He definitely couldn't handle a dead one. But *two*?

I watch as her parents finally look at each other, *really* look at each other, a teary silence settling over them.

Stella's been taking care of all of us. Her mom, her dad, *me.* I keep counting down to eighteen, to being an adult, holding the reins. Maybe it's time I actually acted like it. Maybe it's time I took care of myself.

I blink, looking over to Barb, her eyes widening at the same time as mine.

Uh-oh. I'm like a deer caught in the headlights, unsure if I should bolt or just get what's coming to me. I hesitate for too long and she storms over, grabbing my arm and pulling me down the hall to the elevator. "Oh, hell no."

I stay silent as the elevator doors slide open and she drags me inside.

She presses the button for the third floor, again and again and again, shaking her head. I can feel the anger literally radiating off her.

"Look, Barb. I know you're mad, but she was scared. I just had to see her. . . ."

The doors slide shut and she spins around to look at me, her face like thunder. "You could *kill* her, Will. You could ruin any chance she has for new lungs."

"She's in more danger under that anesthesia than she is with me," I fire back.

"Wrong!" Barb shouts as the elevator slows to a stop, the doors opening. She storms out and I follow behind her, calling after her.

"What is your deal, Barb?"

"Trevor Von and Amy Presley. Young CFers, just like you and Stella," Barb says, turning on her heel to face me. "Amy came in with B. cepacia."

Her eyes are serious, so I close my mouth before I make

one of my usual comments and let her keep talking. "I was young, about Julie's age. New at this. New at *life*."

She looks past me, staring into a different time.

"Trevor and Amy were in love. We all knew the rules. No contact, six feet apart. And I"—she points to herself—"I let them break the rules because I wanted them to be happy."

"Let me guess, they both died?" I ask, knowing the ending long before she tells it to me.

"Yes," she says, looking me dead in the eyes, fighting back tears. "Trevor contracted B. cepacia from Amy. Amy lived for another decade. But Trevor? He got ripped off the top of the transplant list and lived only two more years after the bacteria tanked his lung function."

Shit.

I swallow, looking from her to Stella's room, just past the nurses' station. The list of things that can happen to us CFers, the ghost stories we're told, is pretty much endless. But hearing Barb talk about Trevor and Amy, it doesn't feel like a ghost story at all.

"It was on *my* watch, Will," she says, pointing at herself and shaking her head adamantly. "I'll be damned if it's gonna happen again."

With that, she turns and walks away, leaving me speechless.

I look over to see Poe standing in his doorway, his expression unreadable. He heard the whole thing. He opens his mouth to say something, but I hold up my hand, cutting him off. I make a beeline for my room, closing the door loudly behind me.

I grab my laptop from my nightstand and sit down on the bed. My fingers hover over the keyboard, and then I search it. I search *B. cepacia.*

Words jump out at me.

Contamination.

Risk.

Infection.

With just a cough, with just a single touch, I could ruin her entire life. I could ruin any chance she has for new lungs. I could *hurt* Stella.

I knew it, I guess. But I didn't really *see* it.

The thought of that makes every bone in my body ache. Worse than surgeries, or infections, or waking up on a bad morning barely able to breathe. Even worse than the pain of being in the same room as her and not being able to touch her.

Death.

That's what I am. That's what I am to Stella.

The only thing worse than not being able to be with her or be around her would be living in a world that she didn't exist in at all. Especially if it's my fault.

CHAPTER 15

STELLA

"Time to wake up, honey," a voice says, somewhere far in the distance.

It's my mom's voice, closer now. From right beside me.

I take a deep breath, the world swinging into focus, my head foggy. I blink as her face comes into view, my dad standing beside her.

I'm alive. I made it.

"There's my Sleeping Beauty," she says, and I rub my eyes groggily. I know I just woke up, but I am *exhausted.*

"How do you feel?" my dad asks, and I respond with a sleepy groan, smiling at the both of them.

There's a knock on the door and Julie pushes it open, coming in with a wheelchair to take me down to my room. And my *bed.* Thank goodness.

I swing my hand into the air, holding up my thumb hitchhiker style, and shout out, "Can I get a ride?"

Julie laughs, and my dad helps me get off the gurney and into the wheelchair. Whatever pain meds I'm on right now are *strong*. I can't feel my face, let alone the pain from my G-tube.

"We'll stop by later to check in on you!" my dad says, and I shoot them both a thumbs-up, freezing.

Wait.

We'll.

We'll stop by later to check in on you?

"Did I wake up in an alternate universe?" I grumble, rubbing my eyes and squinting at them.

My mom smiles and strokes my hair comfortingly as she looks over at my dad. "You're *our* daughter, Stella. Always have been, always will be."

These pain meds are *strong*.

I open my mouth to say something, but I'm too stunned and exhausted to string a sentence together. I just nod, my head swinging wildly up and down.

"Go get some sleep, sweetie," my mom says, planting a kiss on my forehead.

Julie takes me down the hall and into the elevator. It's almost impossible to keep my eyes open, my eyelids feeling heavier than a sack of potatoes.

"Phew, Jules, I am *pooped*," I slur, shooting her a side eye and seeing her pregnant belly at eye level just over my shoulder.

The elevator doors open and she wheels me into my room,

locking the tires on the wheelchair. "The skin and tube look much better. You'll be up and around by this afternoon. No crunches, though."

I struggle as she helps me stand slowly and get into bed, my legs and arms feeling like lead weights. She fixes my pillows and tucks me in gently, pulling the covers up over my body.

"You get to hold your own baby," I say, sighing sleepily, sadly.

Julie meets my gaze. She sits down on the edge of my bed, letting out a long sigh. "I'm going to need help, Stella. It's just me." She smiles at me, her blue eyes warm. "Can't think of anyone I would trust more."

I reach out, trying to be as gentle as possible as my exhausted hand *pats* her stomach once, twice.

Nailed it.

I give her a big grin. "I'm going to be the best aunt ever."

Aunt Stella. Me. An aunt? I slump down sleepily, the surgery and the pain meds finally overtaking me. She kisses me on the forehead and leaves, the door gently closing behind her. I sink into my pillow, curling up and pulling my panda closer. I look over at my side table, my eyes slowly clos— Wait! I sit up, grabbing a folded-paper box sitting there, tied with a red ribbon.

I pull the ribbon, and the box unfurls into a handmade, colorful, pop-up bouquet of flowers, the same purple lilacs and pink hydrangeas and white wildflowers as in Abby's drawing suddenly brought to life.

Will.

I smile, putting it gently back down as I fumble around for my phone. I grab it, and it takes everything in me to focus on the screen as I scroll through to Will's number. I hit dial, listening to it ring, my eyes closing as it goes to voice mail. I jump at the beep, my voice slurred when I start speaking. "It's me! Stella. Don't call me, okay? 'Cause I just had surgery and I'm so tired, but call me when you—get this. But no, don't. Okay? 'Cause if I hear your sexy voice, I won't be able to sleep. Yeah. So, call me, okay?"

I fumble with the phone, pressing the end button. I curl up, pulling my blankets closer to my body and grabbing my panda again. I'm still staring at the flowers when I finally drift off to sleep.

My phone starts chirping, pulling me out of my deep, post-surgery sleep. I roll over, my eyes less heavy as they open, and see that Poe is calling me on FaceTime. Fumbling with the screen, I finally press the green button, and his face appears.

"You're alive!"

I grin, rubbing my eyes and sitting up. I'm still sleepy, but the drugs have worn off enough that my head doesn't feel like a paperweight.

"Hey. I'm alive," I say, my eyes widening as they land on

the beautiful bouquet of flowers still on my side table. "The tube's looking good."

Will. I vaguely remember opening the bouquet.

I quickly double-check my text messages. Two from my mom. Three from Camila. One from Mya. Four from my dad. All checking in to see how I'm feeling.

There are none from Will.

My heart falls about twenty stories.

"Have you talked to Will?" I ask, frowning.

"Nope," Poe says, shaking his head. He looks like he wants to say something else, but he doesn't.

I take a deep breath, coughing, my side aching where the skin infection was. Ow. I stretch. The pain is definitely there. But manageable.

I have a message on Instagram, and I swipe to see that it's a reply from Michael that I got while I was sleeping. He messaged me last night to see how Poe was doing, asking about his bronchitis. And—most surprisingly—if he was going to visit his parents in Colombia. I had no idea he was even considering it.

We talked back and forth for close to an hour, about how happy he is that I'm here with Poe at the hospital, about how great Poe is.

How he doesn't understand what went wrong.

He really cares about him.

"Michael DM'd me," I say, glancing up to see Poe's reaction to my words as I toggle back onto FaceTime.

"What?" he asks, surprised. "Why?"

"Asking if you're okay." Poe's expression is unreadable, his dark eyes serious. "He's sweet. Really seems to love you."

He rolls his eyes. "In my business again. Clearly, you've fully recovered."

Poe is missing out on love. Because he's *afraid.* Afraid to go the distance. Afraid to fully let someone into all the crap we have to live with. I know what it's like to have that fear. But that fear didn't stop the scary shit from happening.

I don't want it anymore.

"I'm just saying," I say, shrugging casually, even though my words are serious. "He doesn't care that you're sick."

Michael doesn't care that Poe has CF. He cares that he can't be there for Poe.

When you have CF, you don't know how much time you have left. But, honestly, you don't know how much time the ones you love have left either. My gaze travels to the pop-up bouquet.

"And what's this about visiting your family—you're definitely going, right?"

"Call me when you're off the drugs," he says, glaring at me and hanging up.

I send a quick text to both my parents, telling them to head home and get some rest, since it's already late afternoon and I need to sleep a bit longer. They've been stuck here for hours, and I don't want them waiting for me to wake up when they need to take care of themselves.

They both object, though, and a few minutes later there's a knock on my door, the two of them, *together*, popping their heads in to look at me.

I remember vaguely the "we" from when I first woke up, the two of them a united front for the first time since Abby's death.

"How are you feeling?" my mom asks, smiling at me and kissing my forehead.

I sit up, shaking my head. "Listen, you two should really go, you've been here—"

"We're your parents, Stell. Even though we aren't together, we are still here for you," my dad says, taking my hand and squeezing it. "You always come first. And these past few months . . . we definitely haven't showed that."

"These past few months have been tough on all of us," my mom says, sharing a look of understanding with him. "But it's not on you to make us feel better, okay? We're your parents, honey. More than anything, we want you to be happy, Stella."

I nod. Never in a million years would I have expected this.

"By the way," my dad says, plunking down in the chair next to my bed. "The soup was *great.* Say what you want about cafeteria food, but they make a *mean* broccoli cheddar."

My mom and I look at each other, smiles giving way to deep belly laughs that I have to suppress so my new G-tube doesn't hurt. The sadness stays put, but I feel an ounce of the weight on my shoulders slowly drift away, and I inhale, breathing a little easier than I have in a long time. Maybe this surgery wasn't the worst thing after all.

I doze off for a little longer after my parents leave, sleeping off the last bit of the fogginess, and when I wake up an hour later, I'm fully out of the anesthesia haze. I slowly sit up, stretching, the pain from my surgery pulling at my side and chest. The pain meds are wearing off too.

I lift up my shirt to take a look. My skin is still raw and sore from surgery, but the area around my G-tube already looks about a million times better.

My eyes fall on the pop-up bouquet and I grin excitedly, carefully standing up and taking a deep breath. The air struggles in and out of my lungs, and I take my portable oxygen off my bedside table, putting the nose cannula in and turning it on to give them a hand.

I reply to Mya and Camila to let them know I'm awake and not to worry. I'm as good as new. Or, at least back to 35 percent.

I still have to dish to them about what just happened with my parents, but they're getting on a boat and I have somewhere I need to be too.

Getting changed, I move slowly and carefully, pulling on a pair of leggings and a tie-dye T-shirt that Abby got me when she went to the Grand Canyon. I catch a look at myself in the mirror, the dark circles under my eyes looking deeper than they've been in months. I brush my hair quickly and put it into a neat ponytail, frowning when it doesn't look as good as I hoped it would.

I put it back down, nodding in contentment at my reflection as my hair falls gently around my shoulders. Grabbing my makeup bag from the bottom of my drawer, I put on some mascara and lip gloss, smiling at the idea of Will seeing me not just alive, but with makeup on, his blue eyes gazing at my gloss-covered lips. Would he want to kiss me?

I mean, we could *never*, but would he want to?

I blush, shaking my head as I send a quick text to him, telling him to meet me in the atrium in ten minutes.

Pulling the strap of my portable oxygen farther up on my shoulder, I take the quick way, going up the elevator and across the bridge into Building 2, then back down the stairs into the atrium, which takes up the entire back half of the building. I sit down on a bench, gazing around at all the trees and plants, a stone fountain trickling softly behind me.

My heart pumps eagerly at the thought of seeing him in just a few short minutes.

Excited and anxious, I pull out my phone, checking the time. It's been ten minutes since my text to Will and he still isn't here.

I send him another text: I'm here. Did you get my message? Where are you?

Another ten minutes goes by. And then another.

Maybe he's taking a nap? Or maybe his friends came for a visit and he hasn't gotten a chance to check his phone?

I spin around when I hear the door open behind me, smiling, excited to finally see—Poe. What is Poe doing here?

He looks at me, his face serious. "Will's not coming."

"What?" I manage to get out. "Why isn't he coming?"

"He doesn't want to see you. He's not coming."

He doesn't want to *see* me? What? Poe holds out a pack of tissues, and I stretch to grab them, frowning in confusion.

"He told me to tell you that this little thing between the two of you is over."

The shock and hurt change into anger, deep and real, clawing at my stomach. Why would he sing Abby's song to me before surgery? Why would he sneak into pre-op and risk getting caught? Why would he make me a handmade bouquet of flowers if this "little thing" between us was over?

A frustrated tear rolls down my face and I rip the pack of tissues open. "I hate him," I say, wiping my eyes angrily.

"No, you don't," Poe says, leaning against the wall and looking at me. His voice is soft but matter-of-fact.

I laugh, shaking my head. "He probably had a good laugh about the crazy control freak in 302, huh? He didn't want to tell me all this himself so he could laugh in my face? How unlike him."

I sniff, and pause because even though I'm angry, that

feels wrong. This doesn't make sense. "Is he okay? Did something happen?"

Poe shakes his head. "No, nothing happened." He pauses, his eyes traveling to look behind me, at the trickling fountain. "Well, let me revise that."

He meets my eyes. "Barb happened."

He tells me about what he overheard in the hallway, how Barb confronted Will about us, how being together would kill the both of us.

I don't even let him finish. How long will I live my life afraid of what-ifs? My life revolves around an obsessive regimen and percentages, and given that I was just in surgery, the risk never seems to go down. Every minute of my life is what-if, and it would be no different with Will.

But I can already tell one thing. It'll be different without him.

I storm past Poe, pushing through the heavy doors and up the stairs and across the bridge to the elevators.

"Stella, wait!" he calls after me, but I need to see Will. I need *him* to tell me that this is what he wants.

I pound the elevator button, over and over again, but it's taking too long. I look both ways to see Poe coming after me, his face confused. I keep moving to the stairwell, coughing and clutching at my side, the pain from the surgery making my head spin. I push open the door and speed down the stairs.

I make it back to our floor, throwing open the double

doors and banging on the door to room 315. I glance at the nurses' station, relieved to find it empty.

"Will," I gasp, my chest heaving. "I'm not leaving until you talk to me."

There's silence. But I know he's in there.

Poe's footsteps pound on the floor of the hallway, stopping six feet from me.

"Stella," he gasps out, shaking his head, his own chest heaving from trailing after me.

I ignore him and knock again, louder this time. "Will!"

"Go away, Stella," his voice says through the door. There's a pause, then, "Please."

Please. There's something about the way he says it. A longing, deep and strong.

I'm tired of living without really living. I'm tired of wanting things. We can't have a lot of things. But we could have this.

I know it.

"Will, just open the door so we can talk."

A full minute goes by, but then the door cracks open, just enough so that I can see his shadow on the tile floor. When he doesn't come out, I start to step back against the far wall, like I always do.

"I'll back up, okay? All the way to the wall. I'll be far enough away." Tears start to fill my eyes again, and I swallow, forcing them back.

"I can't, Stella," he says softly, and I see his hand grip the doorframe through the crack.

"Why not? Will, come on—"

He cuts me off, his voice firm. "You know I want to. But I can't." His voice catches in his throat, and I know.

I know in that moment that this "little thing" between us isn't over. It's just starting.

I take a step toward the door, wanting to see him now more than I want to even breathe. "Will . . ."

The door closes in my face, the latch clicking into place. I stare at it, stunned, feeling all the wind get knocked clean out of me.

"Maybe it's better this way," a voice says from behind me.

I turn around to see Poe, still standing there, his eyes sad but his voice resolute.

"No." I shake my head. "No. I can figure this out. I . . . have to figure this out, Poe. I just . . ."

My voice trails off and I look down. There has to be a way.

"We're not normal, Stell," Poe says softly. "We don't get to take these kinds of chances."

I whip my head up, glaring at him. Of all the people to be against us. "Oh, come on! Not you, too."

"Just admit what's really going on here," he fires back, matching my frustration with his own. We stare at each other and he shakes his head. "Will's a rebel. He's someone who takes risks, just like Abby."

My insides turn to ice. "You want to tell me what to do with my life?" I shout back. "What about yours? You and Tim. You and Rick. Marcus. *Michael.*"

His jaw tightens. "Don't go there, Stella!"

"Oh, I can *keep* going there!" I clap back. "They all knew you were sick and they loved you anyway. But *you* ran, Poe. Not them. *You.* Every time." I lower my voice, shaking my head, challenging him. "What are you afraid of, Poe?"

"You don't know what you're talking about!" he shouts back at me, his voice laced with fury, and I know I struck a chord.

I take a few steps closer, looking him right in the eye. "You've ruined every chance at love that ever came your way. So, please, keep your advice to yourself."

I whirl around, marching off to my room, the air still buzzing with anger. I hear his door slam shut behind me, loud and reverberating all around the hallway. I head into my room and throw my door shut with the same amount of force.

I stare at the closed door, my lungs heaving up and down as I struggle to catch my breath, everything silent except for the hiss of my oxygen and the pounding of my heart. My legs give way, and I slide down onto the floor, every fiber of my body suddenly giving out from the surgery and from Will and from Poe.

There has to be a way. There is a way. I just need to figure it out.

• • •

The next few days blur together. My parents come to visit, separately, and then together again on a Wednesday afternoon, and they're being, if not friendly, at least cordial to each other. I FaceTime Mya and Camila, but only for short bursts of time in between their Cabo-ing. I roam the hospital, checking off treatments on my app halfheartedly and going through the motions of my regimen, just like I'm supposed to, but it doesn't feel as satisfying.

I've never felt more alone.

I ignore Poe. Will ignores me. And I keep trying to think of a way to fix this, but nothing comes.

Thursday evening, I sit on my bed, Googling *B. cepacia* for the millionth time, and then there's a clink against my door. I sit up, frowning. What could that be? I walk over and slowly open the door to see a jar resting against the doorframe with a fancy handwritten label: BLACK WINTER TRUFFLES. I bend down, picking it up to see a pink Post-it note sitting on top. I peel it off, reading: "You're right. For once. 😉"

Poe. Relief floods through me.

I break out into my first real smile in four days. Peering down the hallway, I see his door click shut. I grab my phone, dialing his number.

He answers in half a ring.

"Buy you a donut?" I ask.

We meet in the multipurpose lounge, and I grab him a package of his favorite chocolate minidonuts from the vending machine, tossing them to him on his love seat.

He catches them, giving me a look as I buy a pack for myself. "Thanks."

"Welcome," I say, sitting opposite from him, his eyes like daggers.

"Bitch," he shoots back.

"Asshole."

We grin at each other, our fight officially over.

He opens the package, pulling out a donut and taking a bite. "I *am* afraid," he admits, meeting my eyes. "You know what someone gets for loving me? They get to help me pay for all my care, and then they watch me die. How is that fair to anyone?"

I listen to him, understanding where he's coming from. I think most people with a terminal illness have struggled with this. With feeling like a burden. I know I've felt like that with my parents more times than I can count, especially these past few months.

"Deductible. Meds. Hospital stays. Surgeries. When I turn eighteen, no more full coverage."

He takes a deep breath, his voice catching. "Should that be Michael's problem? Or my family's? It's my sickness, Stella. It's *my* problem."

A tear rolls down his cheek, and he wipes it quickly away. I lean forward, wanting to comfort him, but as always I'm six feet away.

"Hey," I say, giving him a big smile. "Maybe you can get Will to marry you. He's loaded."

Poe snorts, his voice teasing. "He's not picky. He likes *you.*"

I throw a donut at him, hitting him square in the chest.

He laughs before his face gets serious again. "I am sorry. About you and Will."

"Me too."

I swallow, my eyes focusing on a bulletin board just past his head, filled with papers and notices and—a hygiene notice. It's made up of intricate cartoon drawings, each one instructing people on the proper way to hand wash or the correct way to cough in public.

I jump up as an idea starts to take shape.

My to-do list just grew by one.

CHAPTER 16

WILL

I dangle my legs off the side of the roof and listen to her voice mail over and over and over again, just to hear her voice on the other end. Her room is dark except for her desk light, and I see her furiously typing away on her computer, her long brown hair pulled into a messy bun.

What could she be doing this late at night?

Is she still thinking about me?

I look up, watching as a gentle flurry of snow starts to fall, landing on my cheeks and my eyelids and my forehead.

I've been on the roof of dozens of hospitals through the years. I've looked down at the world below and experienced this same feeling at every single one. Longing to be walking through the streets or swimming in the ocean or living life in a way I've never really gotten the chance to.

Wanting something that I couldn't have.

But now what I want isn't outside. It's right here, close

enough to touch. But I can't. I didn't know it was possible to want something so bad you could feel it in your arms and your legs and in every breath you take.

My phone goes off and I look down to see a notification from her app, a tiny pill bottle emoji dancing away.

Bedtime meds!

I can't even explain why I'm still doing it. But I take one more long look at her and stand, walking over to the stairwell door and grabbing my wallet before it slams shut. I climb slowly down the stairs and back to the third floor, making sure no one is in the hallway before sneaking back in and down to my room.

Going over to the med cart, I take my bedtime pills with chocolate pudding, just like she taught me. I stare at the drawing I did earlier of myself as the Grim Reaper, the blade of my scythe reading "LOVE."

You still doing okay? Hope texts me.

Sighing, I pull off my hoodie and send a text back, fudging the truth a bit. Yeah, I'm fine.

I set up my G-tube feeding and get into bed. I grab my laptop off my bedside table and open YouTube, clicking solemnly on a suggested video of Stella's that I've already seen, because I am just that pathetic right now.

Hope and Jason would not even recognize me.

Hitting mute, I watch the way she tucks her hair behind her ear when she's concentrating, and the way she throws her head back when she laughs, and the way she crosses her arms in front of her chest when she's nervous or upset. I watch the way she looks at Abby, and her parents, even the way she jokes around with her friends—but, most of all, I watch the way that people love her. I see it in more than just her family. I see it in Barb's eyes, and Poe's eyes, and Julie's eyes. I see it in every doctor and every nurse and every person who comes into her path.

Hell, even the comments aren't the garbage fire most YouTube videos get.

Soon I can't watch anymore. I close my laptop and shut off my light, and lie there in the darkness, feeling every heartbeat in my chest, loud and resolute.

The next day I stare out the window, watching the afternoon winter sun slowly near the horizon as the steady vibrating of my AffloVest thrums away at my chest. I check my phone, surprised to see a text from my mom, checking in with me, instead of my doctors, for the first time since her visit almost two weeks ago: Heard you've been doing your treatments. Glad to see you've come around.

Rolling my eyes, I toss my phone onto my bed, coughing a wad of mucus into the bedpan I'm holding. I glance over at my door as an envelope slides underneath it, my name written on the front of it.

I know I shouldn't be excited, but I unhook the AffloVest

anyway, jumping up to grab it off the floor. Ripping the envelope open, I pull out a carefully folded piece of paper, opening it all the way up to reveal a cartoon drawing done entirely in crayon.

A tall boy with wavy hair is facing a short girl, black crayon labeling them as Will and Stella. I smile as I notice the tiny pink hearts floating above their heads, chuckling at the giant arrow in between reading "FIVE FEET AT ALL TIMES" in big, bright-red letters.

She clearly didn't inherit the same art skills as Abby, but it's cute. What exactly is she trying to say? And *five* feet? It's six and she knows it.

My laptop dings behind me, and I race over to it, swiping my fingers across my trackpad to see a new text. From Stella.

There's nothing there except a link to a YouTube video. When I click on it, it takes me to Stella's newest video, posted exactly three minutes ago.

"B. cepacia—A Hypothetical."

I smile warily at the title, watching as Stella waves to the camera, her hair in the messy bun I saw last night from the roof, a pile of items carefully laid out on her bed in front of her.

"Hi, everyone! So, there's something a little different I want to talk to you about today. Burkholderia cepacia. The risks, the restrictions, the rules of engagement, and how to successfully say it ten times fast! I mean, come on, that is *quite* a name."

I watch, confused. "All right, so, B. cepacia is a hardy bacterium. It's so adaptive that it actually feeds on penicillin instead of being attacked by it. So our first line of defense is . . ." She pauses, reaching down to pick up a pocket-size bottle of liquid and holding it up to the camera. "Cal Stat! This is *not* your average Purell. This is a hospital-grade hand sanitizer. Apply liberally and often!"

She snaps on a pair of blue latex gloves, wiggling her fingers to get them comfortably onto her hands. "Next up is good old-fashioned latex gloves. Tried and true, and used for protection in"—she looks down, clearing her throat and examining the pile of items on her bed—"all kinds of activities."

All kinds of activities? I shake my head, a smile creeping onto my face. *What* is she doing?

Next, I watch as she pulls out a handful of surgical face masks, hanging one around her neck. "B. cepacia thrives best in saliva or phlegm. A cough can travel six feet. A sneeze can travel up to *two hundred miles per hour*, so don't let one fly in mixed company."

Two hundred miles per hour. Wow. Good thing I don't have allergies, or we'd all be done for.

"No saliva also means no kissing." She takes a deep breath, looking right at me through the camera. "Ever."

I exhale, nodding solemnly. That's a major bummer. The thought of kissing Stella is . . . I shake my head.

My heart rate practically triples at just the thought of it.

"Our best defense is distance. Six feet is the golden rule," she says, before bending over to pick up a pool cue from next to her bed. "This is five feet. Five. Feet."

I glance over to the cartoon drawing of us, the red bubble letters jumping out at me. "FIVE FEET AT ALL TIMES."

Where the hell did she get a pool cue?

She holds it out, staring at it with remarkable intensity. "I did a lot of thinking about foot number six. And, to be honest, I got mad."

She looks up at the camera. "As CFers, so much is taken away from us. We live every single day according to treatments, pills."

I pace back and forth, listening to her words.

"Most of us can't have children, a lot of us never live long enough to try. Only other CFers know what this feels like, but we're not supposed to fall in love with each other." She stands up, determined. "So, after all that CF has stolen from me—from *us*—I'm stealing something back."

She holds up the pool cue defiantly, fighting for every one of us. "I'm stealing three hundred and four point eight millimeters. Twelve whole inches. One fucking foot of space, distance, length."

I stare at the video in total admiration.

"Cystic fibrosis will steal no more from me. From now on, I am the thief."

I swear I hear a cheer somewhere in the distance, rallying

in agreement with her. She pauses, looking directly into the camera. Looking directly at *me.* I stand there, stunned, jumping as there's three loud knocks on my door.

I yank open the door and there she is. Live.

Stella.

She holds the pool cue out, the tip of it touching my chest, her full eyebrows rising in challenge. "Five feet apart. Deal?"

Exhaling, I shake my head, her speech from the video already making me want to close the space between us and kiss her. "That's going to be hard for me, I'm not gonna lie."

She looks at me, her eyes intent. "Just tell me, Will. Are you in?"

I don't even hesitate. "So in."

"Then be at the atrium. Nine o'clock."

And with that, she lowers the pool cue, spinning around and walking back off to her room. I watch her go, feeling excitement overtaking the doubt sitting heavy in the pit of my stomach.

I laugh as she holds up the pool cue in victory like at the end of *The Breakfast Club,* smiling back at me before going inside room 302.

I take a deep breath, nodding.

Cystic fibrosis will steal no more from me.

CHAPTER 17

STELLA

"Why didn't I pack anything nice?" I cry to Poe, who is leaning against the doorway helping me. I sling pajamas and sweatpants and baggy T-shirts out of my drawers as I desperately search for something to wear tonight.

He snorts. "Right. Because you usually pack for a hot hospital romance?"

I pull out a pair of skimpy, silky boxers, eyeing them. I *couldn't.* Could I? I mean, it's this or a pair of baggy flannel sweatpants I got as a hand-me-down from Abby.

"I've got nice legs, right?"

"Don't even think about it, ho!" he says, giving me a look before the both of us burst out laughing.

I think of my friends on their last night in Cabo, and for the first time since I got here I don't wish I were there. I wish they were here, helping me get ready. If anything, I'm glad I'm *not* miles away right now.

I look over at the clock on my bedside table. Five o'clock. I have four hours to figure something out. . . .

I walk through the doors of the atrium, noticing a vase filled with white roses. I snag one, bending the stem until it snaps, and put it behind my ear. Glancing at my reflection in the glass of the door, I smile, nervously giving myself a quick once-over. My hair is down, the front tied back with the ribbon from the pop-up flowers from Will, and I'm wearing the skimpy silk boxers and a tank top, despite Poe's laughter.

I look pretty nice considering I pulled it together from the worst date wardrobe in history.

It is nice to know that Will definitely likes me for me. I mean, he's pretty much exclusively seen me in pajamas or a hospital gown, so he clearly isn't in this for my good looks and impeccable Fall 2018 Hospital Collection wardrobe.

I fix the blue latex gloves on my hands, double-checking that the Cal Stat is still hanging off the strap on my portable oxygen.

Sitting down on a bench, I look through a side door leading to the children's playroom, a wave of nostalgia hitting me. I used to sneak in here to play with the non-CFers growing up. Well, and Poe. The atrium hasn't changed much through the years. The same tall trees, the same brightly colored flowers, the same tropical fish tank right by the doors, where Poe and I got in trouble with Barb for throwing donut crumbs to the fish.

The atrium may not have changed much since I've been coming to Saint Grace's Hospital, but I sure have. I've had so many firsts at this hospital, it's hard to count them all.

My first surgery. My first best friend. My first chocolate milk shake.

And now, my first *real* date.

I hear the door slowly creak open, and I peer around the corner to see Will.

"Over here," I whisper, standing up to hold out the pool cue to him.

A huge smile breaks out on his face, and he takes the other end of the pool cue in his gloved hand, a travel-size bottle of Cal Stat shoved into his front pocket.

"Wow," he says, his eyes warm as he looks me over, making my heart do somersaults inside my chest. He's wearing a blue plaid flannel that hugs his thin body, making his eyes look an even brighter shade of blue. His hair is neater. Combed, but still maintaining that messiness that is unbelievably hot.

"That's a beautiful rose," he says, but his eyes are still on my exposed legs, the dip in my silky tank top.

I blush, pointing at the rose tucked behind my ear. "Oh, this rose? This one? Up here?"

He pulls his eyes away, giving me a look that no other boy has given me before. "That's the one," he says, nodding.

I tug on the pool cue, and we walk through the atrium toward the main lobby. He looks to the side, noticing the vase full of white roses sitting on the table, his eyes crinkling as he smiles. "You stealing roses, Stella? First a whole foot and now *this*?"

I laugh, reaching up to touch the rose tucked behind my ear. "You got me. I stole it."

He pulls at the other end of the pool cue, shaking his head. "Nah, you gave it a better home."

CHAPTER 18

WILL

I can't take my eyes off her.

The red ribbon in her hair. The rose tucked behind her ear. The way she keeps looking at me.

I don't feel like any of this is real. I've never felt this way about anyone before, mostly because all my relationships before were centered on living fast and dying young and always leaving for a new hospital. I didn't stay anywhere or with anyone long enough to really fall for anyone.

Not that I even would have, given the chance. None of them was Stella.

We stop in front of a big tropical fish tank, and it takes everything in me to look away from her at the brightly colored fish behind the glass. My eyes follow an orange-and-white fish swimming around and around the coral at the bottom of the tank.

"When I was really little, I used to just stare at these

fish, wondering what it would feel like to be able to hold my breath long enough to swim like they do," she says, following my gaze.

That surprises me. I knew she had been coming to Saint Grace's for a while, but I didn't know she'd been here when she was a little kid.

"How young?"

She watches as the fish swims upward before diving back down to the bottom. "Dr. Hamid, Barb, and Julie have taken care of me since I was six."

Six. Wow. I can't even imagine being in one place that long.

We walk through the doors into the main lobby, the large staircase looming in front of us. She looks back at me, tugging on the pool cue and nodding to them. "Let's take the stairs."

The stairs? I look at her like she's actually insane. My lungs burn from just the thought of it as I remember my exhaustion from my trips up to the roof. Not exactly sexy. If she wants this date to last longer than an hour, there is no way we're about to walk up those stairs.

Her face breaks into a smile. "I'm kidding."

We roam the almost empty hospital, the hours blurring together as we walk, talking about our family and our friends and everything in between, the pool cue swinging back and forth between us. We head up to the open bridge between Buildings 1 and 2 and walk slowly across, craning our necks to look through the glass ceiling at the stormy gray night sky, the snow falling steadily onto the roof of the bridge and all around us.

"What about your dad?" she finally asks, and I shrug.

"He cut and ran when I was little. Having a sick kid wasn't in his plan."

She watches my face, trying to see my reaction to those words. "It happened so long ago, sometimes it feels like I'm just telling someone else's story. Another person's life that I've memorized."

You don't have time for me, I don't have time for you. Simple as that.

She moves on when she sees I mean what I'm saying. "And your mom?"

I attempt to hold the door open for her, which is apparently *very* tricky to do when you're holding a pool cue and need to be five feet apart at all times, but I'm a gentleman, dammit.

I sigh, giving her the brief, generic response. "Beautiful. Smart. Driven. And focused on me and me alone."

She gives me a look that says this isn't going to cut it. "After he left, it's like she decided to care enough for two people. Sometimes I feel like she doesn't see me. Doesn't know me. She just sees the CF. Or now the B. cepacia."

"Have you talked to her about it?" she asks.

I shake my head, shrugging the topic away. "She's not

there enough to listen. She's always dictating, then out the door. But starting in two days, when I'm eighteen, I make the decisions."

She stops short and I'm yanked back as my end of the pool cue is jerked in her direction.

"Hold up. Your birthday is in two days?"

I smile at her, but she doesn't smile back. "Yep! Lucky number eighteen."

"Will!" she says, stomping her foot, upset. "I don't have a present for you!"

Can she get any cuter?

I tap her leg with the pool cue, but for once I'm not kidding. There's something I actually want. "How 'bout a promise, then? To stick around for the next one?"

She looks surprised, and then nods. "I promise."

She takes me to the gym, and the motion-activated lights flicker on as she pulls the other end of the pool cue past the exercise gear and to a door in the far corner that I never bothered to explore before.

Looking both ways, she flicks open the lid to a keypad and punches in a code.

"So you pretty much have the run of the place, huh?" I ask as the door unlocks with a click, a green light shining through the keypad.

She smirks, giving me a look as she closes the lid. "One of the perks of being the teacher's pet."

I laugh. Well played.

The warmth of the pool deck hits me as we open the door, my laugh echoing around the open space. The room is dim, except for the lights in the pool, shining bright as the water ripples around them. We take off our shoes and sit on the edge. The water is cool at first despite the heat of the room, but slowly warms up as we move our feet back and forth.

A comfortable silence settles over us, and I look over at her, a pool cue's length away.

"So, what do you think happens when we die?"

She shakes her head, smirking. "That's not very sexy first-date talk."

I laugh, shrugging. "Come on, Stella. We're terminal. You have to have thought about it."

"Well, it is on my to-do list."

Of course it is.

She looks down at the water, moving her feet in circles. "There's one theory I like that says in order to understand death, we have to look at birth."

She fidgets with the ribbon in her hair as she talks.

"So, while we're in the womb, we're living *that* existence, right? We have no idea that our *next* existence is just an inch away."

She shrugs and looks at me. "Maybe death is the same. Maybe it's just the next life. An inch away."

The next life just an inch away. I frown and think it over.

"So, if the beginning is death and death is also the end, then what's the real beginning?"

She raises her thick eyebrows at me, not amused by my riddle. "Okay then, Dr. Seuss. Why don't you tell me what you think."

I shrug and lean back. "It's the big sleep, baby. Peace out. Blink. Done and done."

She shakes her head. "No way. There's no way that Abby just 'blinked' out. I refuse to believe it."

I'm silent, watching her, wanting to ask the burning question I've held on to since I figured out Abby died. "What happened?" I ask. "To Abby?"

Her legs stop circling in the pool, the water still swirling around her calves, but she tells me. "She was cliff diving in Arizona and she landed wrong when she hit the water. Broke her neck and drowned. They said she didn't feel any pain." She meets my gaze, her expression troubled. "How could they know, Will? How could they know if she felt pain? She was always there for me when I was in pain, and I wasn't there to do the same."

I shake my head. I have to fight all my instincts, which tell me to reach out and take her hand. I don't know what to say. There's just no way to know. She looks back at the water, her eyes glazed over, her mind far away, on the top of a cliff in Arizona.

"I was supposed to be there. But I got sick, just like I

always do." She exhales slowly, with effort, her eyes unblinking, focused on a point at the bottom of the pool. "I keep imagining it, over and over, wanting to know what she felt or thought. Because I can't know that, she never stops dying for me. I see it over and over and over again."

I shake my head, tapping her leg with the pool cue. She blinks, looking over at me, her eyes clearing. "Stella, if you had been there, you still wouldn't know."

"But she died alone, Will," she says, which is something that I can't deny.

"But we all die alone, don't we? The people we love can't go with us." I think about Hope and Jason. Then my mom. I wonder if she'll be more upset to lose me, or to lose to the disease.

Stella swirls her legs in the water. "Do you think drowning hurts? Is it scary?"

I shrug. "That's how we're going to go, isn't it? We drown. Just without the water. Our own fluids will do the dirty work."

I see her shiver out of the corner of my eye, and give her a look. "I thought you weren't afraid to die?"

She sighs loudly, looking over at me exasperatedly. "I'm not afraid of *being* dead. But the actual dying part. You know, what it feels like?" When I stay silent, she keeps talking. "You're not afraid of any of it?"

I swallow my usual instinct to be sarcastic. I want to be real with her. "I think about that very last breath. Sucking for air. Pulling and pulling and getting nothing. I think about my chest muscles ripping and burning, absolutely useless. No air. No nothing. Just black." I look at the water, rippling around my feet, the detailed image in my head familiar and sinking into the pit of my stomach. I shudder, shrugging and smiling at her. "But, hey. That's only on Mondays. Otherwise, I don't dwell on it."

She reaches out, and I know she wants to take my hand. I know because I want to take hers, too. My heart slows a beat, and I see her freeze halfway, curling her fingers into her palm and lowering her hand.

Her eyes meet mine, and they're filled with understanding. She knows that fear. But then she gives me this small smile, and I realize we're here in spite of all that.

Because of her.

I fight for a deep breath, watching the glow from the pool as it plays against her collarbone and her neck and her shoulders.

"God, you're beautiful. And brave," I say. "It's a crime I can't touch you."

I lift the pool cue, wishing more than anything it was my fingertips against her skin. Gently, I trace the end of it up her arm, over the sharp angle of her shoulder, slowly making my way to her neck. She shivers underneath my "touch," her eyes locked on mine, a faint red blooming in her cheeks as the pool cue climbs.

"Your hair," I say, touching where it falls over her shoulders.

"Your neck," I say, the pool light brightening her skin.

"Your lips," I say, feeling the dangerous pull of gravity between us, daring me to kiss her.

She looks away, suddenly shy. "I lied, the day we met. I haven't had sex." She takes a breath that's sharp, touching her side as she speaks. "I don't want anyone to see me. The scars. The tube. There's nothing sexy about—"

"Everything about you is sexy," I say, cutting her off. She looks at me and I want her to see it in my face. I mean, *look* at her. "You're perfect."

I watch as she pushes the pool cue away, standing, trembling. She reaches for her silk tank top, her eyes fixed on mine as she pulls it slowly off to reveal a black lace bra. She drops the tank top onto the deck of the pool, my jaw going with it.

Then she slips down her shorts, stepping carefully out of them and straightening up. Inviting me to look.

She's knocked the wind right out of me. I try to take in as much as I can, hungrily making my way up and down her body, gazing at her legs and her chest and her hips. The light dances against the raised battle scars on her chest and stomach.

"Dear god," I manage to get out. I never thought I could be jealous of a pool cue, but I want to feel her skin against mine.

She smiles coyly at me before sliding into the pool, going

completely under the water. She stares up at me, her long hair fanning out around her like she's a mermaid. I tighten my grip on the pool cue as she comes up gasping for air.

She chuckles. "What was that? Five seconds? Ten?"

I close my mouth, clearing my throat. It could've been a year for all I know. "I wasn't counting. I was staring."

"Well, I showed you mine," she says, daring me.

And I always take a dare.

I stand up, unbuttoning my shirt. Now she's the one looking at me. And she doesn't say anything, but her lips are parted, not frowning, not pitying.

I walk to the pool steps, sliding out of my pants, and stand there for a moment in just my boxers, the water and Stella calling to me. Slowly, I step into the pool, our eyes locked on each other's as we struggle for air.

For once, it has nothing to do with our CF.

I sink under the water and she follows me, small bubbles floating to the surface as we look at each other across the washed-out world underneath the water, our hair floating up and around us, pulling toward the surface, the lights casting shadows off our thin bodies.

We smile at each other, and even though there are a million reasons why I shouldn't, looking at her now, I can't help feeling like I'm falling in love with her.

CHAPTER 19

STELLA

We leave the pool, our hair slowly drying as night turns into early morning. We walk past things I've seen a million times in my years at Saint Grace's. Dozing security guards, and surgeons angrily shaking the broken vending machine by the lobby, the same white tile floors and the same dimly lit hallways, but everything seems different with Will next to me. It's like seeing everything for the first time. I didn't know it was possible for a person to make old things become new again.

We walk slowly past the cafeteria and stand in front of a huge glass window off to the side, away from any passersby, watching the sky slowly lighten. Everything is still quiet on the other side of the glass. My eyes land on the lights at the park in the distance.

I take a deep breath and point at them. "See those lights?"

Will nods, looking over at me, his hair slicked back from

the pool water. "Yeah. I always look at them when I sit on the roof."

He watches me as I look back at the lights. "Every year Abby and I would go there. She used to call them stars because there are so many." I smile, laughing. "My family used to call me Little Star."

I hear Abby's voice in my ear, saying my nickname. It hurts, but the pain isn't as sharp. "She'd make a wish and she'd never, ever tell me what it was. She used to joke that if she said it out loud, it would never come true." The tiny pinpoints of light twinkle in the distance, calling out to me, as if Abby is out there now. "But I knew. She wished for new lungs for me."

I breathe in and out, feeling the ever-present struggle of my lungs to rise and fall, and I wonder what it would be like with new lungs. Lungs that, for a short while, would completely change life as I know it. Lungs that would actually work. Lungs that would let me breathe, and let me run, and give me more time to really live.

"I hope her wish comes true," Will says, and I lean my head on the cold glass, glancing over at him.

"I hope my life wasn't for nothing," I say, my own wish on those twinkling lights.

He gives me a long look. "Your life is everything, Stella. You affect people more than you know." He touches his chest, putting his hand over his heart. "I speak from experience."

My breath fogs up the glass of the window, and I reach up,

drawing a big heart. We look at each other in the reflection of the glass, and I feel the gravity of him, pulling at me across the open space. It tugs at every single part of me, my chest and my arms and my fingertips. I want to kiss him more than I want absolutely anything.

Instead, I lean over, kissing his reflection on the glass.

He reaches up slowly, touching his mouth with his fingertips, like he felt it, and we turn to face each other. I look over at him as the sun slowly crests the horizon, casting a warm glow onto his face, his eyes bright and filled with something brand new but somehow familiar.

My skin starts to prickle.

He takes a small step toward me, his gloved hand sliding slowly up the length of the pool cue, his eyes cautious as my heart begins to race. I move to step closer, to steal back a few more inches, to be just that much nearer to him.

But my phone goes off, chirping away over and over, and the magic of the moment floats away like a balloon. I grab my phone from my back pocket and see a text from Poe, feeling a mix of sadness and relief as Will and I pull away from each other.

SOS.

Barb is looking for you two!!!

WHERE ARE YOU GUYS?

Oh my god. Panic fills every part of me, and I look up at Will, my eyes wide. If she finds us together, we'll never have a second date. "Oh no. Will. Barb's looking for us!"

What are we going to do? We couldn't be farther from our wing.

He looks panicked too for a fraction of a second, and then he pulls himself together, his eyebrows furrowing as he goes into full-on damage-control mode. "Stella, where will she look for you first?"

My mind races. "The NICU!"

The west entrance. Barb will be coming in from the other side. If I book it, I can maybe make it there in time.

My head snaps over to the elevators, and I see the doors slowly closing. Grimacing, I lean the pool cue against the wall, and bolt for the stairwell as Will books it in the opposite direction, back to our floor.

Putting one foot after the other, I chug up the stairs, my arms and legs starting to burn as I drag my body up to the fifth floor. Yanking my portable oxygen farther up on my shoulder, I head down the empty corridor. My feet slap against the floor noisily, my breathing coming in frantic gasps.

This is so bad. Barb will *kill* me. Well, first Will, then definitely me.

My lungs feel like they are on fire as I slam my body against the door with a large red five printed on it, the west entrance to the NICU swimming into view. I try to suck in as much air as I possibly can, coughing desperately as I flip open a keypad, my hands shaking too much to type in the numbers.

I'm going to get caught. I'm too late.

I grab my right hand with my left, steadying it enough to type 6428. *NICU*. The door unlocks with a click, and I throw myself onto an empty couch, my head swimming as I slam my eyes shut, pretending to sleep.

Not even a second later the east entrance door bursts open, and I hear footsteps, then smell Barb's perfume as she stops short right next to me. My chest burns as I try to control my breathing, trying desperately to look tranquil while my body yearns for air.

I feel a blanket fan out over me, and then hear her steps slowly leaving, the east entrance door opening and closing behind her.

I sit bolt upright, coughing, my eyes filling with tears as a blinding pain shoots across my chest and all over my body. The pain gradually fades, my vision clearing as my body gets the air it needs. The amount of relief I feel right now is matched only by the amount of adrenaline coursing through my body.

I pull out my phone, sending a thumbs-up emoji to Will. He responds half a second later with: I CAN'T BELIEVE WE DIDN'T GET CAUGHT.

I laugh, sinking down into the warm couch, the whirlwind of last night still making my heart float miles above the hospital.

There's a knock on my door, jolting me awake from my uncomfortable nap sprawl in the hideous green armchair by the window. I rub my eyes sleepily as I check my phone, squinting at the screen.

It's already one o'clock. Which would explain the three million texts from Camila and Mya and Poe asking about how last night went.

Last night.

I smile at just the thought of it, feeling a wave of happiness overtake me. Standing, I shuffle over to the door and pull it open, confused when there's nobody on the other side. That's odd. Then I look down, noticing a cafeteria milk shake sitting on the floor, a note resting underneath it.

Bending down, I pick it up, smiling as I read: "Poe said you like chocolate. Vanilla is obviously the better flavor, but I'll let it slide because I like you."

He even took the time to draw a cartoon podium, with a vanilla ice-cream cone beating out chocolate and strawberry for the first-place medal.

I laugh, looking down the hall to see Will outside his door, wearing a face mask and gloves. He pulls the face mask down and makes a face as Barb rounds the corner. He winks at me and pushes open the door to his room, quickly disappearing inside before she sees him.

I hide the milk shake and note behind my back, slapping on a big smile. "Morning, Barb!"

She looks up from a patient chart, eyeing me suspiciously. "It's afternoon."

I nod, slowly stepping back inside. "Sure, right. Afternoon." I gesture with my free hand. "All this snow, you know, makes it hard to tell . . . what time of day it is."

I roll my eyes, closing the door before I can say anything more ridiculous.

We lie low for the rest of the day so we don't make Barb more suspicious of us. We don't even risk Skyping or texting. I make a big show of reorganizing my med cart, secretly slipping notes under Will's door every time I'm in the hallway to get more supplies.

Will heads to the vending machine about a dozen times, his replies coming with every new bag of chips or candy bar.

"When is date number two?" he writes, and I smile, glancing to my notebook at what I've actually spent my day working on.

My plan for his birthday tomorrow.

CHAPTER 20

WILL

I watch my mother sleepily from the edge of my bed as she argues back and forth with Dr. Hamid. As if screaming about it will somehow help change the results of my stats. There's been no change from the Cevaflomalin.

Not exactly the best birthday present.

"Maybe there's an adverse drug interaction. Something keeping the new drug from working as it should?" she fires back, her eyes practically frantic.

Dr. Hamid takes a deep breath, shaking her head. "The bacteria in Will's lungs are deeply colonized. Antibiotic penetration into lung tissue requires time for any drug." She points at my daily IV of Cevaflomalin. "This drug is no different."

My mom takes a deep breath, gripping the edge of my bed. "But if it's not effective—"

Not again. I'm not leaving again. I stand up, cutting her

off. "Enough! It's over, Mom. I'm eighteen now, remember? I'm not going to any more hospitals."

She spins around to look at me, and I can tell she's ready for this moment, her eyes filled with anger. "Sorry I'm ruining your fun by trying to keep you alive, Will! Worst mother of the year, right?"

Dr. Hamid slowly backs toward the door, knowing this is her cue to leave. My eyes flick back to my mother, and I glare at her. "You know I'm a lost cause, don't you? You're only making it worse. No treatment is going to save me."

"Fine!" she fires back. "Let's stop the treatments. Stop spending the money. Stop *trying*. Then what, Will?" She stares at me, exasperated. "You lie down on a tropical beach and let the tide take you? Something stupid and poetic?"

She puts her hands on her hips, shaking her head. "Sorry, but I don't live in a fairy tale. I live in the real world, where people solve their . . ."

Her voice trails off, and I take a step forward, raising my eyebrows, daring her to say it. "Problems. Go ahead, Mom. Say it."

It's the word that sums up what I've always been to her.

She exhales slowly, her eyes softening for the first time in a long time. "You are not a problem, Will. You are my *son*."

"Then be my mom!" I shout, my vision going red. "When was the last time you were that, huh?"

"Will," she says, taking a step closer to me. "I'm trying to help you. I'm trying to—"

"Do you even know me at all? Have you looked at a single one of my drawings? Did you know there's a girl I like? I'll bet you didn't." I shake my head, the rage pouring out of me. "How could you? All you see of me is my fucking disease!"

I point at all the art books and magazines stacked on my desk. "Who is my favorite artist, Mom? You have no idea, do you? You want a problem to fix? Fix how you look at me."

We stare at each other. She swallows, collecting herself and reaching over to take her purse from off the bed, her voice soft and steady. "I see you just fine, Will."

She leaves, closing the door quietly behind her. Of course she left. I sit down on my bed, frustrated, and look over to see an elaborately wrapped gift, a big red ribbon carefully tied around it. I almost throw it out, but instead I grab it, ready to see just what she could possibly think I'd want. I rip off the ribbon and the wrapping paper to reveal a frame.

I can't understand what I'm seeing. Not because I don't recognize it. Because I do.

It's a political cartoon strip from the 1940s. An original of the photocopy I have hung up in my room.

Signed and dated and everything. So rare, I didn't even think any still existed.

Shit.

I lie back on my bed, grabbing my pillow and putting it over my face, the frustration I was feeling toward her transferring to myself.

I resented so much the way she was always looking at me that I didn't realize I was doing the exact same thing.

Do I know where she's off to now? Do I know what *she* likes to do? I've been so focused on how I want to live my own life, I've entirely forgotten she has one.

It's me.

Without me, my mom is all alone. All this time I thought she only saw my disease. A problem you fix. But, instead, she was looking right at me, trying to get me to fight against it alongside her, when all I did was fight *her* tooth and nail. All she wanted was for me to stay and fight, when all I kept doing was getting ready to leave.

I sit up, pulling down the photocopy and replacing it with the framed, one-of-a-kind original.

She wants the same thing as Stella. More time.

She wants more time with me.

I push back from my desk, ripping out my earbuds as I go. I've spent the past two hours drawing, trying to shake off my confrontation with my mom.

I know I should say something. Reach out, with a call or a text, but I can't help but still feel a little pissed. I mean, this is a two-way street, and she definitely hasn't been doing a perfect job on her end either. If she would have just shown me she was listening, even a little . . .

I sigh, grabbing a chocolate pudding cup and my afternoon pills from off my med cart and dutifully taking them. Pulling out my phone, I sit down on the edge of my bed and aimlessly scroll through my messages on Instagram to see a bunch of birthday wishes from my old classmates.

Nothing from Stella, yet. She hasn't sent me anything since last night, when I asked about a second date.

I give her a call on FaceTime, grinning when she picks up. "I'm free!"

"Wha—?" she starts, her eyes widening. "Oh right, happy birthday! I can't believe I didn't—"

I wave my hand, cutting her off. No biggie. "You busy? Wanna take a walk? Barb's not around."

She pans the phone over a bunch of textbooks sitting in front of her. "I can't right now. I'm studying."

My heart sinks. Really? "Yeah, okay. I just thought that maybe . . ."

"How about later?" she asks, the view panning back up to her.

"My friends are visiting later," I say, shrugging sadly. "It's cool. We'll figure something out." I look sheepishly at her. "I was just, you know, missing you."

She smiles at me, her eyes warm, her face happy.

"That's all I wanted to see! That smile." I run my fingers through my hair. "All right. I'll let you get back to your books."

I hang up, lying back on my bed and chucking my phone onto my pillow.

Barely a second later it starts to ring. I grab it, answering it without even looking at the screen to see who is calling. "I knew you'd change your—"

"Hey, Will!" a voice says on the other end. It's Jason.

"Jason! Hey," I say, a little bummed that it isn't Stella, but still glad to hear from him. This thing with Stella has been happening so fast, I haven't really had a chance to catch him up.

"Something came up," he says, but he sounds weird. "I'm sorry, man. We can't make it over there today."

Seriously? First Stella and now Jason and Hope? Birthdays are sort of in short supply for me. But I shake it off. "Oh, yeah, okay. I totally get it." He starts apologizing, but I cut him off. "Seriously, dude, it's fine! Not a big deal."

I hang up, sighing loudly, and as I'm sitting up, my gaze falls on my nebulizer. I grab the albuterol and shake my head, mumbling, "Happy birthday to me."

I jolt awake from an evening nap as my phone chirps, a message coming in. I sit up, my eyes focus on the screen, and I swipe right to read a text from Stella.

HIDE AND SEEK. You're it. XOXO S.

I roll out of bed, confused but curious as I slide into my white Vans and throw the door open. A bright-yellow balloon almost smacks me in the face, its long string tied to the doorknob. I squint, realizing that there's something sitting inside the balloon at the very bottom.

A note?

I double-check that the coast is clear before stomping on the balloon to pop it. A boy walking back to his room with an open bag of chips jumps about ten feet at the noise, the chips flying out of the bag and scattering on the floor. I quickly grab the rolled-up Post-it note from inside, unfurling it to see a message written in Stella's neat handwriting.

Start where we first met.

The NICU! I sneak down the hallway, past the boy resentfully picking up his potato chips, and take the elevator up to the fifth floor. I sprint across the bridge into Building 2, dodging nurses and patients and doctors, and head through the double doors into the east entrance of the NICU. Looking around, my head flies in every direction, searching for another—there! Tied to an empty crib behind the glass is another bright-yellow balloon. I carefully tiptoe inside, fumbling with the knot on the string to untie the balloon.

Jesus, Stella. Is she a freaking sailor?

I finally get it undone, and creep back out into the hallway, looking both ways before— *POP*.

I unfurl the note to read the next clue.

Roses are red. Or are they?

I frown, staring at the message. "Or are they" . . . Oh! I picture her face from the other night, the white rose tucked carefully behind her ear. The vase. I head straight for the atrium, sprinting down the steps of the main lobby and into the glass-enclosed room. Pushing open the doors, I see the yellow balloon floating, its string tied tightly to the vase.

I wave to the security guard, who peers at me suspiciously as I rip the balloon off the vase, struggling to catch my breath, my lungs protesting all this running. I grin at him, popping the balloon loudly, and shrugging sheepishly in explanation. "It's my birthday."

I grab the message from the inside, opening it up to read:

If only I could hold my breath for this long . . .

I barely finish reading before I spin around to the tropical fish tank, the bright oranges and yellows of the fish jumping out at me as my eyes scan furiously around the outside of the tank for a balloon.

Did I get it wrong?

I think again. The pool.

I hurry out of the room, heading to the gym in Building 1, the last note clutched in my hand as I go. Pushing open the doors to the gym, I move past all the empty exercise equipment and see the door to the pool is promisingly propped open with a chair. Stepping inside, I breathe a sigh of relief when I see the yellow balloon floating on top of the water, a few feet from the edge.

Looking to the side, I see the pool cue from Friday.

Sweeping the cue under the balloon, I grab the string and pull the balloon out of the water, noticing a tug at the end as something on the bottom of the pool weighs it down.

Pulling it up, I laugh, recognizing the bottle of Cal Stat from Stella's video.

I use the pool cue to pop the balloon, sifting through the dead remnants to get to the message inside.

At exactly forty-eight hours from our first date . . .

I flip the note over, frowning, but that's it. I check my watch. Eight fifty-nine. One more minute until it's forty-eight hours from our first— My phone chirps.

I swipe to see a picture of Stella, looking cute as hell in a chef's hat and holding a yellow balloon, a big smile on her face. The message reads: . . . our second date begins!

I frown at the picture, zooming in to see where she could possibly be. Those metal doors are just about everywhere in this hospital. But wait! I slide to the right edge of the picture to see a corner of the milk-shake machine in the cafeteria. I power walk to the elevator, taking it up to the fifth floor and down the hall and across the bridge into Building 2. I hop on another elevator and swing back down to the third floor, where the cafeteria is, catching my breath and smoothing out my hair in the reflection in the brushed-stainless-steel walls, pool cue still in hand.

I casually swing around the corner to see Stella leaning against the door to the cafeteria, a look of pure joy filling her face when she sees me. She's wearing makeup, her long hair pulled away from her face with a headband.

She looks beautiful.

"I thought you'd never find me."

I hold out the pool cue, and she takes the other end, pushing open the door and leading me across the dark cafeteria.

"It's late, I know, but we had to wait until the cafeteria closed."

I frown, looking around. "We?"

She looks back at me as she stops in front of a pair of frosted-glass doors, her expression unreadable as she punches a code into the keypad. With a click, the doors open, and a bunch of voices yell out, "Surprise!"

My jaw drops. Hope and Jason, but also Stella's friends, Mya and Camila, just back from Cabo, sit at a completely set table covered in a hospital sheet, white candles sitting on either end of it casting a warm glow on a basket filled with fresh bread and a perfectly chopped salad. There are even medicine cups with red-and-white Creon pills set in front of three seats at the table.

I am completely stunned.

I look from the table to Stella, knocked speechless.

"Happy birthday, Will," she says, tapping my side gently with the pool cue.

"He's real!" Camila (or is it Mya?) says, and I laugh as Hope rushes over to me, giving me a big hug.

"We felt so terrible ditching you!" she says.

Jason hugs me too. Patting me on the back. "But your girlfriend over there tracked us down through your Facebook page and convinced us to surprise you."

Mya and Camila high-five at his word choice, making Stella shoot them a glare before glancing over at me. We share a look. *Girlfriend.* That has an awfully nice ring to it.

"This is definitely a surprise," I say, looking around at all of them, so full of appreciation.

Poe appears, wearing a face mask, a scrub cap, and gloves, and swings a pair of tongs in the air. "Hey! Food's almost ready!"

We sit down, keeping a safe distance between all CFers. Stella at one end, me at the other, and Poe in the middle with Hope and Jason on either side of him. Mya and Camila sit on the opposite side of the table, securing the distance between Stella and me. I smile, looking around the table at everyone as we dig into the salad and the bread. My heart feels so full, it's disgusting.

I look across the table, smiling at Stella, and mouth a "thank you." She nods, blushing and looking down.

Girlfriend.

• • •

Poe serves the most beautiful-looking lobster pasta dish I have ever seen, garnished with basil leaves and fresh Parmesan and even truffles! Everyone stares at it in complete awe.

"Where did all this come from?" I ask him as my stomach grumbles noisily.

"Right here!" Poe says, gesturing behind him to the kitchen. "Every hospital has a VIP kitchen where they keep the good stuff for celebrities, politicians." He shrugs. "You know, the important people."

He grabs a glass off the table, raising it. "Tonight, birthday boy, it's for you! *Salud!*"

Everyone raises their glass. *"Salud!"*

I look across the table at Stella, winking. "Too bad I'm allergic to shellfish, Poe."

Poe stops dead midserve and slowly looks over at me. I crack a grin, shaking my head. "Kidding, kidding!"

"I almost threw a lobster at you," Poe says, laughing.

Everyone laughs with us, and we all dig in. It is by far the best pasta I have ever eaten, and I've been to Italy. "Poe!" I say, holding up a forkful. "This is incredible!"

"You're going to be the best chef in the world one day," Stella says in agreement, and Poe gives her a big smile, blowing a kiss in her direction.

Pretty soon, we're all swapping stories. Jason tells a story about how we convinced our entire school to wear nothing but underwear the day before summer vacation two years ago. Which was especially impressive considering we'd get detention if our tie wasn't straight.

That's the one thing I don't miss about school. The uniforms.

Stella starts talking about all the mischief she and Poe used to get into here at the hospital, from trying to steal the milk-shake machine in the cafeteria to holding wheelchair races in the children's ward.

It sounds like I'm not the only one Barb nearly killed on a regular basis.

"Oh, have I got one for you guys!" Poe says, looking over at Stella. "Halloween that one year?"

She starts cracking up already, her eyes warm as she shakes her head at him.

"We were, what, Stella? Ten?"

Stella nods, taking over the story. "So, we put on sheets and . . ." Poe starts making ghostly *OOOOHHH* sounds, holding out his arms and floating around the room. "We snuck into the dementia ward."

You've got to be kidding me.

I start coughing because I'm laughing so hard. I slide my chair back from the table, waving my hand for them to continue while I catch my breath.

"No!" Jason says. "No, you didn't."

"Oh, man," Poe says, wiping away a tear. "It was absolute

pandemonium, but it was by far the best Halloween ever. We got in so much trouble."

"It wasn't even our idea!" Stella starts to say. "Abby . . ."

Her voice trails off, and I watch her struggle to speak as I apply some Cal Stat from my travel bottle. She meets my gaze from across the table, and I see how hard it is for her.

"I miss her," Camila says. Mya nods in agreement, her eyes teary.

"Abby was wild. Free," Poe says, nodding. "She always said she was going to live wide open because Stella wasn't able to."

"And she did," Stella says. "Until it killed her."

The room goes completely quiet. I watch as she meets Poe's gaze, both of them sad but smiling as they share a moment, remembering her.

I wish I could've met her.

"But she lived big. A lot bigger than we do," Poe says, smiling. "She would've loved a clandestine party like this one."

"Yeah," Stella says finally. "She really would have."

I hold up my glass. "To Abby," I say.

"To Abby!" everyone else chimes in, holding up their glasses. Stella looks at me across the table, the look in her hazel eyes by far the best birthday present I could ever get.

CHAPTER 21

STELLA

I lean against the counter, smiling at Poe as he pulls a freshly baked pie out of the oven, totally in his element. He glances up at me, thick eyebrows raised.

"I wanted to see the master at work."

He winks at me, taking his oven mitts off, and I watch as he confidently twirls his chef's knife, deftly slicing the pie into eight even pieces with a flourish.

I clap as he grabs a fresh strawberry and squints. He leans over it, cutting here, snipping there, in absolute and total concentration. He holds it up in his gloved hand after only a few seconds, a big smile on his face. The strawberry is completely transformed into an intricate, beautiful rosette, which he puts on the side of the pie.

My jaw drops open. "Poe! That's incredible."

He shrugs casually. "I've been practicing for next month when Michael and I visit my mom," he says, giving me a look that clearly is telling me this is no big deal.

So, of course, I shriek in excitement. Finally!

"Yep," he says, grinning from ear to ear. "You're right, Stella. He loves me. And these past few weeks without him have been harder than I could've imagined. I love him." He's practically radiating joy. "He's coming for lunch tomorrow. We're gonna go for it."

I almost tackle him with a hug but catch myself before I can close the space between us and do it. I look at the counter, grabbing a kitchen mitt and putting it on so I can reach out and take his hand in mine.

Tears fill my eyes, and I sniff, shaking my head. "Poe. I'm so—"

He rips the kitchen mitt off my hand, smacking it over my head as tears fill his eyes. "*Dios mio!* Don't go all soppy on me, Stella! You *know* I can't let a girl cry alone."

"Happy tears, Poe," I say as we both stand there sniffling. "I'm so happy!" The sound of laughter comes from the other room, and he wipes his eyes.

"Come on! We're missing all the fun!"

Poe carefully carries out his beautifully made pie with a sea of candles sitting on top of it and we all start to sing. I watch Will smiling in the glow of the candlelight, looking around the table at all of us.

"Happy birthday to you. Happy birthday to you. Happy birthday, dear Will. Happy birthday to you!"

And many more. I mouth the words to him. They've never had more feeling behind them than right now.

"Sorry it's a pie!" Poe says, smiling at him. "I'm good, but baking a cake in an hour is definitely out of my league."

"It's amazing, Poe. Thank you so much," Will says, smiling back at him and then eyeing the candles warily. "If I blow them out, then you guys can't eat it."

His eyes flick between me and Poe, and we nod solemnly.

Hope leans over, blowing out the candles. She ruffles Will's hair, smiling at him. "I made a wish for you!"

He smiles back at her, winking. "I hope it involves Stella popping out of a birthday cake in a bikini!"

Everyone laughs and Mya pulls out her phone and a selfie stick, holding her arm out to take a group photo. We crowd together, the best we can while keeping a safe CF distance. The second the camera clicks—*BOOM.*

The frosted-glass door behind us slams open, all of us jumping in shock and spinning around to see . . . *Barb.* Uh-oh. She stares at us, and we stare back at her. Everyone too stunned to say anything.

Poe clears his throat. "Hi, Barb. We thought you were off tonight. Can we make you a plate? Stella's just about to start the entertainment."

Barb must be doing a double today. I'm sure it's not an accident she kept that quiet. She knows me. And she knew it was Will's birthday. Fuck.

She stares at us, speechless, rage overflowing from every feature on her face. She points at the three of us, and my heart goes haywire.

"Up. Now."

We stand slowly, walking over to her. She shakes her head, looking around at us, words failing her.

"Follow me." She starts walking out, swinging through the door and back across the cafeteria.

We shoot small waves good-bye in Hope and Jason and Mya and Camila's direction, before following her out. This is bad. I've seen Barb mad or upset on plenty of occasions. But not like *this.* This is another kind of scary.

We follow her down the hallway. I shoot a worried look over at Will, and he mouths, "It'll be okay." But his smile doesn't quite reach his eyes.

"You're all confined to your rooms while we get respiratory cultures," she says, spinning around to face Will. "And you. You'll be transferred in the morning."

"No!" I say, and her eyes swing over to meet mine. "No, Barb, it wasn't Will's fault—"

She holds up her hand, cutting me off. "You may be willing to gamble with your lives, but I'm not."

There's a thunderous silence, and then Poe laughs. We all look over at him, and he shakes his head, completely unfazed. He meets my eyes and gives me a big smile. "Just like when we were kids—"

"You're not kids anymore, Poe!" Barb shouts, stopping him midsentence.

"We were careful, Barb," he says, shaking his head, his voice serious. "We were safe. Just like *you* taught us to be." He gestures to the distance we're keeping from one another even now.

He coughs. A quick, short cough, and then adds, "I'm sorry, Barb. But it was fun."

She opens her mouth to say something, and then quickly closes it, spinning around to take us the rest of the way to our floor. Nobody says a single word for the rest of the trip. I look over at Will. I want to get closer, but that's exactly what got us into trouble in the first place.

We all go off to our respective rooms, Poe winking at me and Will before ducking inside. Barb giving me a final disappointed look before my door swings shut.

As the clock ticks closer and closer to midnight, I watch Will, fast asleep on the other side of my laptop screen, his face calm, peaceful. I rub my eyes, sleepy from the long day of planning for his party and getting caught by Barb. We don't hang up because we know soon he'll be far away in isolation. No more midnight walks. No more exercise room. No more slipping notes under doors. Nothing.

My eyelids are slowly shutting when an alarm blares over the speaker, jolting me awake.

"Code blue. All available personnel—"

I jump up, running to the door so I can hear the garbled words of the announcement. Oh god. A code blue. Someone's heart has stopped working. And there aren't that many of us on this floor right now.

As I swing open the door, the announcement is repeated again, clearer now that I'm in the hallway.

"Code blue. All available personnel to room 310. Code blue."

Room 310.

Poe. Please tell me he just didn't put the monitor on right again.

I clutch at the wall, the room spinning as a rapid response team pushes a crash cart past me. I see Julie following them into Poe's room, her shift just starting. Barb's voice calls out, somewhere in the distance, "He's not breathing! There's no pulse. We have to move fast."

This can't be happening.

I start to run, stumbling to his room. I see his legs on the floor, his feet falling in two different directions. No. No, no, no.

Barb is covering his body, pushing air into his lungs with a bag valve mask. He isn't breathing. Poe isn't breathing.

"Come on, baby, don't do this to me!" she shouts as another voice yells, "Place defibrillator pads!"

A shape bends over him, cutting open his favorite Colombia soccer jersey, which his mom sent him for his birthday, slapping two pads on his chest. I finally see his face; his eyes are rolled back, his skin blue.

My arms and legs go numb.

"Poe!" I shout, wanting to get to him, wanting him to be okay.

Barb's eyes meet mine and she shouts, "No! Someone get her away from here."

"Massive tension pneumothorax. His lung is collapsing. We need an intubation tray!" a voice yells, and I stare at his unmoving chest, trying to will it to lift.

Breathe. He has to breathe.

Bodies are all around me and I try to shove past them. I need to get to him. I need to get to Poe. I struggle against arms and shoulders, trying to push them away.

"Close that door!" Barb says as hands pull me back out into the hallway. I hear her voice one more time, talking to Poe. "Fight, baby! Fight, goddammit!"

I see Julie, her eyes dark.

Then the door closes in my face.

I stumble back, turning to see Will standing behind me. His face as pale as Poe's was. He reaches out for me, then closes his hands into fists, frustration filling his eyes. I feel like I'm going to be sick. I reach for the wall, sliding down it onto the floor, my breathing coming in short gasps. Will sits down against the wall, five feet away. I wrap my shaking arms around my legs, resting my head on my knees and squeezing my eyes tightly shut. All I see is Poe lying there.

Striped socks.

Yellow soccer jersey.

This can't be real.

He'll come to. He has to come to. He'll sit up and make a joke about eating too much pasta or swooning too hard over Anderson Cooper, and ask if I want to go get a late-night milk shake with him. The same milk shakes we've been having for ten years.

The same milk shakes we need to have together for another decade.

I hear footsteps and lift my head to see Dr. Hamid hurrying down the hallway.

"Dr. Hamid—" I start, my voice croaking out.

"Not now, Stella," she says firmly, pushing open the door. It swings wide and I see him. His face is turned toward me, his eyes closed.

He still isn't moving.

But worse than that is Barb. Barb has her head in her hands. She's stopped trying. No.

They're taking everything off him. The wires. The intubation tubes.

"No!" I hear my voice scream out, my entire body screaming with it. "No, no, no, no!"

I reach up, pulling myself to my feet, and start running back to my room. He's gone.

Poe's gone.

I stumble down the hallway, seeing his eyes the day we first met, seeing him smile at me from his bedroom door, seeing his hand resting in mine through the kitchen mitt just *hours* earlier. My fingers find the handle to my door and I crash through, everything blurring as tears stream down my face.

I spin around to see Will has followed me, and I take a step closer as sobs rack my body, making my rib cage ache as it becomes impossible to breathe. "He's gone. Will, he's gone! Michael, his *parents*, oh my god." I shake my head, clutching at my sides. "Will! He was just about to . . . They'll never see him again."

The realization slams me. "I'll never see him again."

I ball my hands into fists as I pace. "I never even hugged him. Never. Don't touch! Don't stand too close. Don't, don't, don't!" I scream out, hysterical, coughing, dizzy. "He was my best friend and I never hugged him."

And I never will. The feeling is so horribly familiar, I can't stand it. "I'm losing everyone," I gasp out. Abby. Poe. All gone.

"You're not losing me," Will says, his voice soft but determined. He walks toward me, reaching out, his arms almost wrapping around me.

"No!" I shove him away, stepping back, farther and farther,

well past five feet. I press my back against the far wall of the room. "What are you doing?!"

Realization fills his eyes, and he backs away to the door, looking horrified. "Oh, fuck. Stella. I wasn't thinking, I was just—"

"Get out!" I say, but he's already in the hallway, already running back to his room. I slam the door, my head pounding with anger. With fear. I look around the room, and all I see is loss everywhere, making the walls close in on me, closer and closer.

This isn't a bedroom.

I run to the wall, my fingers curling around the edges of a poster. It gives way, tearing down off the hospital wall.

I rip the bedspread off, throwing the pillows across the room. I grab Patches, chucking him at the door. I push all the books and papers and to-do lists off my desk, everything clattering loudly to the ground. I blindly grab at my nightstand, picking up the first thing I can get my hands on and throwing it at the wall.

The glass jar shatters, a sea of black truffles scattering across the floor.

I freeze, watching them roll in every direction.

Poe's truffles.

Everything goes quiet except for my chest heaving in and out, in and out. I sink to my knees, sobs racking my entire body as I try desperately to pick up the truffles, one by one. I look at Patches, toppled over on his side, ragged and worn, all alone on the floor except for a lone truffle, resting against his tattered leg.

His sad brown eyes stare back at me, and I reach out, picking him up. I hug him to my chest, my eyes traveling to Abby's drawing and then to the picture of the two of us.

I stand up shakily and collapse onto my bed, curling up into a tiny ball on the bare vinyl mattress, tears streaming down my face as I lie there, alone.

Sleep comes and goes, my own sobs jolting me awake over and over again into a reality too painful to believe. I toss and turn, my dreams laced with images of Poe and Abby, smiles twisting into grimaces of pain as they melt away into nothingness. Barb and Julie both come in, but I keep my eyes shut tight until they leave again.

Soon I lie awake, staring at the ceiling as the light shifts across my room, everything giving way to numbness as morning drifts into afternoon.

My phone vibrates noisily on the floor, but I ignore it, not wanting to talk to anyone. Will. My parents. Camila and Mya. What's the point? I'll die or they will, and this cycle of people dying and people grieving will just continue.

If this year has taught me anything, it's that grief can

destroy a person. It destroyed my parents. It will destroy Poe's parents. Michael.

And me.

For years I'd been so *okay* with dying. I've always known it would happen. It's been this inevitable thing that I've lived with forever, this awareness that I would die long before Abby and my parents.

I was never, ever ready to grieve, though.

I hear voices in the hall and I push myself up, wading through the wreckage to the door of my room, picking up my phone as I go, feeling it vibrate in the palm of my hand. I drift out into the hallway, heading toward Poe's room, watching as someone goes in with a box. I follow, without really knowing why. When I peer inside, some part of me expects to see Poe sitting in there, looking up at me as I pass by, like this was all a horrible dream.

I can hear him say my name. *Stella.* The way *he* said it, with that look of warmth in his eyes, that smile playing on his lips.

Instead, it's an empty hospital room, a lone skateboard leaning against the bed. One of the few traces that Poe, my wonderful best friend, Poe, had even filled it. And Michael. He sits on the bed, his head in his hands, the empty box next to him. He's come for Poe's things. The Gordon Ramsay poster. The *fútbol* jerseys. The spice rack.

His body is shaking with sobs. I want to say something, to

comfort him. But I don't have the words. I can't reach outside of the deep pit inside me.

So I squeeze my eyes shut, pulling my head away, and keep walking.

As I pass, my fingertips drag along the door to Will's room. The light is on, shining underneath the bottom, daring me to knock. To go to him.

I keep drifting, though. My feet take me up steps and down hallways and through doors until I look up and see the sign for the children's playroom, the breath catching in my throat as I stare at the colorful letters. This was where it all began. Where I played with Poe and Abby, the three of us having no idea we had such little life ahead of us.

So much of that life right here inside this hospital.

I pull at the collar of my shirt, for the first time in all my years at Saint Grace's feeling the whitewashed walls closing in on me, my chest tightening.

I need to get air.

Flying down the hallway, I head back into Building 1, slamming the elevator button until the steel doors slide open, and the elevator pulls me back down to my floor. Yanking open my door, I turn my head to look warily over at my obsessively organized med cart. All I've done for the longest time is take my meds and go through my stupid to-do lists, trying to stay alive for as long as possible.

But why?

I stopped living the day Abby died. So what's the point?

Poe pushed everyone away so he wouldn't hurt them, but it didn't make a bit of difference. Michael is still sitting on his bed, crushed, the weeks they could have had together spiraling through his head. Whether I die now or ten years from now, my parents will be crushed. And all I'll have done is make myself miserable focusing on a few extra breaths.

I slam open my closet door to grab my coat and scarf and gloves, wanting to get away from all of this. I throw my portable O_2 concentrator into a small backpack and head for the door.

Peering into the hallway, I see the nurses' station is empty.

I clutch at the straps of my backpack, turning toward the stairwell at the end of the hall. Walking quickly, I push open the door before anyone can see me, coming face-to-face with the first set of stairs. I climb one by one, each step bringing me closer to freedom, each gasp for air a challenge to the universe. I run, the exhilaration pushing everything else from my mind.

Soon the red exit door is in front of me. I pull out the folded dollar bill of Will's, still in my coat pocket after all this time. Using it to hold the alarm button down, I pull open the door and use a brick leaning against the wall to keep it open.

I step onto the roof and move to the edge to see the world below. I take a deep breath of the biting air and let out a long scream. I scream until my voice gives way to coughs. But it feels good. Looking down, my lungs heaving, I see Will in his room down below. He pulls a large duffel bag onto his shoulder, heading for the door.

He's leaving.

Will is leaving.

I look to the holiday lights in the distance, twinkling like stars, calling out to me.

This time I respond.

CHAPTER 22

WILL

I sit in my chair, waiting for Barb to come to take me to isolation like I deserve. The morning has rolled into afternoon, afternoon into evening, evening into night, and I still haven't heard anything from her, the threat she gave yesterday buried under what has come to pass.

My eyes travel to the clock on my nightstand as another minute ticks by. Every change in the red numbers putting yesterday further in the past.

Putting Poe in the past.

Poe died on my birthday.

I shake my head sadly, remembering his laughter at dinner. He was *fine* and then just like that . . .

I kick myself, the shock and horror that filled Stella's face as she looked at me, the anger as she pushed me away, haunting me for the millionth time today.

Why did I do that? *What was I thinking?*

I wasn't. That's the problem. Stella thought out all the rules and I couldn't just follow them? What's wrong with me? It's only a matter of time before I do something really stupid. Something that gets us both killed.

I'm getting the fuck out of here.

I launch myself out of the chair, grabbing my big duffel from under my bed. I throw open the drawers and shove my clothes into it, clearing everything out as quickly as I can. Calling an Uber, I pack my art supplies and sketchbooks into my backpack, the pencils and the papers all shoved messily inside after the important stuff. I put the framed cartoon from my mom gently on top of the mound in my duffel bag, wrapping it carefully in a shirt, before zipping my bag closed and dropping a pin for the driver to meet me at the east entrance.

I put on my coat and slip out of my room, booking it down the hall to the double doors and down the elevator to the east lobby. Pulling my beanie on, I shove open the door with my side, heading just inside the lobby doors to wait.

Tapping my foot impatiently, I check the status of my car, squinting when I see movement on the other side of the doors. The glass fogs up and I watch as a hand reaches up to draw a heart.

Stella.

I can see her now, in the darkness.

We stare at each other, the glass of the door between us. She's bundled up in a thick green jacket. A scarf is wrapped tightly around her neck, a pair of gloves on her small hands, her backpack slung over her shoulder.

I reach up, pressing my palm to the glass, inside the heart that she drew.

She crooks her finger, telling me to come outside.

My heart jumps. What is she doing? She has to come back inside; it's freezing. I have to go get her.

I push carefully through the door, the cold air hitting me right in the face. Pulling my hat down lower over my ears, I walk over to her, my footsteps crunching noisily as I walk through the perfect blanket of white.

"Let's go see the lights," she says as I stop next to her, the invisible pool cue between us. She's excited. Almost manic.

I look in the direction of the holiday lights, knowing how far they are. "Stella, that's gotta be two miles away. Come back inside—"

She cuts me off. "I'm going." Her eyes meet mine, resolute, and full of something I've never seen there before, something wild. She's going with or without me. "Come with me."

I'm all for being rebellious, but this seems like a death wish. Two kids with barely functioning lungs walking two miles one-way to go look at lights? "Stella. Now isn't the time to be a rebel. Is this about Poe? This is about Poe, isn't it?"

She turns to face me. "It's about Poe. It's about Abby. It's about you and me, Will, and everything we'll never get to do together."

I stay silent, watching her. Her words sound like they could come straight from my mouth, but when I hear them from her, they don't sound the same.

"If this is all we get, then let's take it. I want to be fearless and free," she says, giving me a look, daring me. "It's just life, Will. It'll be over before we know it."

We walk down an empty sidewalk, the streetlights over our heads making the icy patches shine. I try to stay six feet away from her while we walk, our steps slow as we carefully try not to slip.

I peer at the road in the distance and then back at Stella. "Let's get an Uber, at least?" I think of the one that's already on the way.

She rolls her eyes. "I want to walk and enjoy the night," she says, leaning in and grabbing my hand in hers.

I jerk back, but she holds on tight, her fingers lacing through mine. "Gloves! We're good."

"But we're supposed to be six feet—" I start to say as she moves away from me, stretching our arms out but refusing to let go.

"Five feet," she shoots back, determined. "I'm keeping that one."

I watch her for a moment, taking in the look on her face, and let all the fear and nervousness melt away. I'm finally outside a hospital. Going to actually see something instead of looking at it from a roof or a window.

And Stella is right next to me. Holding my hand. And even though I know it's wrong, I can't see how it possibly could be.

I cancel the Uber.

We trudge on through the snow, the lights beckoning to us in the distance, the park border coming slowly closer and closer.

"I still want to see the Sistine Chapel," she says while we walk, her footsteps assertive as she crunches through the snow.

"That'd be cool," I say, shrugging. It's not at the top of my list, but if she's there, I'd go too.

"Where do you want to go?" she asks me.

"Just about everywhere," I say, thinking of all the places I've been but missed out on. "Brazil, Copenhagen, Fiji, France. I want to go on a worldwide trip where I just go to all the places I've been in a hospital at but never got to explore. Jason said if I ever could do it, he'd go with me."

She squeezes my hand, nodding, understanding, the snow clinging to our hands and our arms and our jackets. "Do you like warm weather or cold weather?" I ask her.

She bites her lip, thinking. "I like snow. But, aside from that, I think I prefer warm weather." She looks over at me, curious. "You?"

"I like the cold. Not a huge fan of trudging through it, though," I reply, fixing my beanie and smirking at her. I bend down, scooping up some snow and packing it together. "But I am a huge fan of snowballs."

She holds up her hands, shaking her head and giggling as she steps away from me. "Will. Do *not.*"

Then she scoops up a snowball and with lightning-fast speed pins me right in the chest. I stare at her in shock, dramatically falling to my knees.

"I've been hit!"

She tags me with another one in response, hitting me in the arm with a sniperlike aim. I chase after her, the two of us laughing and chucking snow in each other's direction as we head toward the lights.

Way too soon, we both begin gasping for breath.

I grab her hand in truce as we huff and puff up a hill, turning around to look back at it all when we finally reach the top.

Stella exhales, fog swirling out of her mouth as we look back at the snow and the hospital, far behind us. "Sure looks better behind us."

I give her a look, watching as the snow falls gently onto her hair and face. "Was this on your to-do list? Break out with Will?"

She laughs, the sound happy, real, despite everything. "No. But my to-do list has changed."

She spreads her arms wide and falls back onto the hill, the snow giving way around her, puffing softly as she lands in it. I watch as she makes a snow angel, laughing as her arms and legs move back and forth, back and forth. No to-do list, no suffocating hospital, no obsessive regimen, no one else to worry about.

She's just Stella.

I spread my arms and fall down next to her, the snow molding to my body as I land. I laugh, making a snow angel too, my whole body cold from the snow, but warm from the moment.

We stop and look up at the sky. The stars seem an arm's length away. Bright enough and close enough for us to just reach out and grab them. I look over at her, frowning when I notice a bulge in the front of her coat, on her chest.

Not that I've been looking, but her boobs are *nowhere* near that big.

"What the hell is that?" I ask, poking at the lump.

She unzips her coat to reveal a stuffed panda, lying limply against her chest. I smirk, looking up to meet her eyes. "I can't *wait* to hear this one."

She pulls the panda out of her jacket, holding it up. "Abby gave this to me for my first hospital trip. I've had it with me every time since."

I can see her, young and small and scared, coming into Saint Grace's for the first time, clutching that ratty panda bear. I laugh, clearing my throat. "Well, that's good. 'Cause I didn't want to have to tell you that a third boob's a deal breaker."

She glares at me, but it gives way quickly. She tucks the panda back inside, sitting up to zip the coat back up.

"Let's go see your lights," I say, standing. She tries to join me but jerks back to the ground. Kneeling, I see that the strap of her O_2 concentrator is caught on a root. I reach out, taking the strap off it, and hold out my hand to help her stand back up. She takes it and I pull, her body swinging up, the motion moving her inches away from me.

I look into her eyes, the air coming out of our mouths intermingling in the small space between us, doing what I know our bodies can't. Behind her I see our snow angels, a perfect five feet apart. I let go, quickly stepping back before the dizzying urge to kiss her overwhelms me again.

We keep walking, finally making it into the park and to the giant pond, the lights just a little bit farther. I watch as the moonlight glints off the frozen surface, dark and beautiful. Looking back, I see Stella breathing heavily, struggling to catch her breath.

"You okay?" I ask, taking a step closer.

She nods, looking past me and pointing. "Let's take a breather."

I glance behind me to see a stone footbridge, turning back to grin at Stella's pun. We walk slowly toward the small bridge, edging carefully along the shoreline of the pond.

Stella stops short, her foot reaching slowly out to touch the ice, and she gradually puts more and more weight on it, testing it out beneath her shoe.

"Stella, don't," I say, picturing her going clean through it into the freezing water beneath.

"It's frozen solid. C'mon!" She gives me a look. The same

look I've seen all night tonight: brave, mischievous, daring.

Reckless comes to mind too. But I push that aside.

If this is all we get, then let's take it.

So I take a deep breath, taking her challenge, and grab her hand as we slide onto the ice together.

CHAPTER 23

STELLA

For the first time in a long time, I don't feel sick.

I grab on to Will's hands as we slip across the surface of the ice, laughing as we struggle to keep our balance. I squeal as I lose mine, letting go of his arms so I don't drag him down with me, and I fall hard on my butt.

"You good?" he asks, laughing harder.

I nod happily. Better than good. I watch as he takes off at a run, whooping as he slides across the ice on his knees. Watching him makes the hurt from Poe less blinding, filling my heart up to the brim, even though it's still in pieces.

My phone rings in my pocket, and I ignore it like I have for most of the day, squinting into the distance at Will as he skitters across the pond. The phone finally stops, and I slowly stand, but then it starts chirping loudly, texts coming in one after the other.

I pull out my phone, annoyed, looking down to see my

screen filled with messages from my mom, from my dad, from Barb.

I expect to see more messages about Poe, but different words jump out at me.

LUNGS. THREE HOURS UNTIL THEY ARRIVE. WHERE ARE YOU???

Stella. Please reply! LUNGS ARE ON THEIR WAY.

I freeze, the air sucking straight out of my current shitty lungs. I look across the pond at Will, watching as he spins slowly around and around and around. This is what I wanted. What Abby wanted. New lungs.

But I look across the pond at Will again, the boy I love, who has B. cepacia and will never get the opportunity in front of me.

I stare at my phone, my mind whirring.

New lungs means hospital and meds and recovery. It means therapy, and potential for infection, and enormous pain. But, most important, it means I'd be apart from Will now more than ever. Isolation, even, to keep the B. cepacia far away from me.

I have to choose now.

New lungs?

Or Will?

I look up at him and he smiles at me so wide that it's not even a contest.

I shut my phone off and launch myself across the ice, sliding and skidding my way over, before crashing at full force into him. He grabs on to me, barely managing to hold on and keep us from slamming into the ice.

I don't need new lungs to feel alive. I feel alive *right now.* My parents said they wanted me to be happy. I have to trust I know what that is. They're going to lose me eventually, and I can't control that.

Will was right. Do I want to spend all my time left swimming upstream?

I push off him and try to spin, throwing my arms out, my face turned toward the starry sky. Twirling around and around on the slick ice, I hear his voice.

"God, I love you."

The way he says it is so soft and real and the most wonderful thing.

My arms drop and I stop spinning, turning to face him, my breathing coming in short gasps. He holds my gaze, and I feel the same pull I've always felt toward him, an undeniable gravity that dares me to close the gap between us. To step across every inch of the five feet.

So this time, I do.

I run to Will, our bodies colliding, our feet giving way as we tumble to the ice, laughing as we land together. I pull his arms around me, resting my head on his chest as the snow falls around us, my heart beating so loud, I'm almost sure he can hear it. I look up at him as he leans in. Each magnetic breath he takes pulling me closer.

"You know I want to," he whispers, and I can almost feel it. His lips meeting mine, cold from the snow and the ice, but absolute perfection. "But I can't."

I look away and rest my head on his coat, watching the snow fall. Can't. *Can't.* I swallow the familiar feeling that pulls at my chest.

He's silent again, and I feel his lungs rising and falling underneath my head, a sigh escaping his lips. "You scare me, Stella."

I look up at him, frowning. "What? Why?"

He looks into my eyes, his voice serious. "You make me want a life I can't have." I know exactly what he means.

He shakes his head, his face somber. "That's the scariest thing I've ever felt."

I think back to when we met, then him teetering on the edge of the roof.

He reaches out, his gloved hand gently touching my face, his blue eyes dark, serious. "Except maybe this."

We're silent, just looking at each other in the moonlight.

"This is disgustingly romantic," he says, giving me a lopsided smile.

"I know," I say. "I love it."

Then we hear it. *Criiick, crack, crick.* The ice groans beneath us. We jump up, laughing, and scramble together, hand in hand, to solid ground.

CHAPTER 24

WILL

"What's your dream place to live?" I ask her as we walk slowly back around to the footbridge, her gloved hand resting inside of mine.

We wipe away the fresh snow on the bridge's railing and hop up, our legs swinging in time with one another.

"Malibu," she says, setting the oxygen concentrator next to her as we look out at the pond. "Or Santa Barbara."

She would pick California.

I give her a look. "California? Really? Why not Colorado?"

"Will!" she says, laughing. "Colorado? With our lungs?"

I grin, shrugging as I picture the beautiful landscape of Colorado. "What can I say? The mountains are beautiful!"

"Oh no," she says, sighing loudly, her voice teasing. "I love the beach and you love the mountains. We're doomed!"

My phone chirps, and I reach into my pocket to see who it's from. She grabs my hand, trying to stop me.

I shrug. "We should at least let them know we're okay."

"Some rebel you turned out to be," she fires back at me, trying to snatch my phone from my hand. I laugh, freezing when I see my screen filled with texts from my mom.

This late at night?

I pull Stella's hand off to see every message is exactly the same: LUNGS FOR STELLA. GET BACK NOW.

I swing my legs around, jumping up, excitement filling me from head to toe. "Oh my god! Stella, we have to go *right now*!" I grab her hand, trying to pull her off the railing. "Lungs—they have lungs for you!"

She doesn't budge. We need to get back ASAP. Why isn't she moving? Doesn't she understand?

I watch her face as she stares off at the lights, completely unfazed by what I just said. "I haven't seen the lights yet."

What the *fuck*?

"You knew?" I ask, shock hitting me like a tractor trailer. "What are we *doing* out here, Stella? These lungs are your chance for a real life."

"New lungs? Five years, Will. That's the shelf life on them." She snorts, glancing over at me. "What happens when those lungs start to fail? I'm right back to square one."

This is all my fault. The Stella from two weeks ago would never be this stupid. But now, all thanks to me, she's about to throw everything away.

"Five years is a lifetime to people like us, Stella!" I shout back, trying to get her to see. "Before the B. cepacia, I would've *killed* for new lungs. Don't be stupid." I pull my phone out, starting to dial. "I'm calling the hospital."

"Will!" she shouts, moving to stop me.

I watch in horror as her cannula tubing catches again on a gap in the stone footbridge, her head jerking back as she loses her balance. She tries to grab the slippery railing ledge, but her hand slides right off and she goes plummeting down.

I try to grab ahold of her, but she slams onto the ice, landing on her back, the concentrator landing with a plunk next to her.

"Stella, shit! Are you okay?" I shout, about to launch myself over the side to her unmoving body.

And then she starts laughing. She's not hurt. Oh, thank god. She's not hurt. I shake my head, relief filling my chest.

"That was some—"

There's a loud crack. I see her scramble, but there's no time.

"Stella!" I call out as the ice shatters beneath her, sucking her in, the dark water swallowing her whole.

CHAPTER 25

STELLA

I thrash, icy water all around me as I try to swim to the surface. My coat is so heavy, the water clings to it, dragging me farther and farther down into the deep. I frantically unzip it, starting to slide out of it when I see Patches, floating away. My lungs burn as I gaze up at the light from the hole that I fell through, the thin cord from the oxygen concentrator a guide to the surface.

But then I look over to Patches.

My body sinks deeper and deeper, the cold pushing the air out of my lungs, bubbles pouring out of me and up to the surface.

I go for the panda, reaching desperately for him, my fingertips grazing his fur. I cough, the last of my oxygen leaving my body, my head pounding, and the water fills my lungs.

My vision blurs and darkens, the water changing in front of my eyes, slowly morphing into a black sky, tiny pinpoints of light appearing.

Stars.

The stars from Abby's drawing. They swim toward me, surrounding me, and circling all around me. I float among them, watching as they twinkle.

Wait.

This isn't right.

I blink, and I'm back in the water, strength filling my body as I pull with everything in me back to the top. A hand reaches out to me, my fingertips wrapping desperately around it as I'm heaved effortlessly out of the water.

I lie there, gasping, and sit up, looking around.

Where's Will?

Reaching up, I feel my hair. Dry. I touch my shirt and my pants. Dry. I lay my palm flat on the ice, expecting to feel the cold. But . . . nothing. Something is wrong.

"I know you miss me, but this is taking it a little far," a voice says from beside me. I look over, taking in the curly brown hair, hazel eyes identical to mine, the familiar smile.

Abby.

It's Abby.

I don't understand. I throw my arms around her, hugging her to make sure she's real. She's really there. She's—wait.

I pull back and look around me, at the frozen pond, at the stone footbridge. "Abby. Am I . . . dead?"

She shakes her head, squinting. "Eh . . . not quite."

Not *quite*? I am so happy to see her, but the relief at her words overwhelms me. I don't want to die yet.

I want to actually *live* my life.

We both hear a splash somewhere in the distance. I turn, looking for the source of the sound, but don't see anything. What was that noise?

I strain my ears and that's when I hear it, like an echo, somewhere in the distance.

His voice.

It's Will's voice, ragged, coming between sharp, shallow breaths. "Hold on, Stella!"

I look at Abby, and I know she hears it too. We look down as my chest starts to slowly expand and fall, expand and fall, over and over and over again.

Like I'm getting CPR.

"Not . . . now. Come . . . on, not now. Breathe," his voice says, clearer now.

"What's happening?" I ask her, watching as the view in front of me starts to slowly change. Will. His silhouette begins to form, close enough to touch.

He's leaning over a body.

My body.

I watch as he shivers, coughing, his body swaying as he starts to collapse. Every single breath is a struggle, and I watch as he gasps for air, trying desperately to fill his lungs.

And every breath he gets, he gives to me.

"He's breathing for you," Abby says as my chest expands again.

With each breath he blows into my lungs, the view in front of me grows more and more vivid. I can see his face turning blue, every breath painful.

"Will," I whisper, watching as he struggles to push the air through my body.

"He really loves you, Stell," Abby says, watching. As the scene sharpens, she fades.

I turn to her, frantic, feeling again the loss that keeps me up at night. The unanswered question.

Abby smiles at me, shaking her head, already far ahead of me. "It didn't hurt. I wasn't scared."

I take a deep breath, letting out a relieved sigh that I've been holding for more than a year now. My chest heaves suddenly, and I begin to cough, water pouring out of my mouth.

I watch as my body, just a few feet away, does the exact same thing.

Abby smiles wider now. "I need you to live, okay? Live, Stella. For me."

She starts to fade and I panic. "No! Don't go!" I say, grabbing on to her.

She holds me tight, hugging me close to her, and I can smell the warm, flowery scent of her perfume. She whispers in my ear, "I'm not going far. I'll always be here. Just an inch away. I promise."

CHAPTER 26

WILL

My throat is on fire.

My lungs are done.

One more time. For Stella.

"Not . . . now. Come . . . on, not now. Breathe," I beg her, the cold pounding at my body as I hold her face in my hands, pushing all my air into her lungs.

It hurts so bad, I can hardly stand it.

My vision begins to fade, black swimming in from the edges, slowly overtaking everything until all I see is Stella's face surrounded by a sea of black.

I have nothing left to give. I have nothing left to—*no.*

I straighten, desperately pulling in one more short breath, knowing deep in my chest that it is the last breath I will ever get.

And I give it to her. I give everything I have to her, the girl that I love. She deserves that.

I push every bit of air in my body into her lungs, collapsing on top of her, no idea if it was enough, hearing the sirens of the ambulance I called blare in the distance. Water trickles over my head as my hand finds hers and I finally let the darkness consume me.

CHAPTER 27

STELLA

I feel something pricking at my arm.

My eyes fly open, my head spinning as my vision slowly comes back, bright lights overhead. But not the holiday lights, wrapping beautifully around the trees in the park. They're the fluorescents of the hospital.

Then faces block them.

Mom.

Dad.

I sit up, pushing out from under the blankets, and look over to see Barb. She's standing next to the ER nurse, who is drawing blood from my arm.

I try to push the nurse's hands away, try to get up, but I'm too weak.

Will.

Where is Will?

"Stella, calm down," a voice says. Dr. Hamid leans over me.

"Your new lungs—"

I rip the oxygen mask off, looking for him. Dr. Hamid tries to get it back over my face, but I turn away, squirming out of her reach. "No, I don't want them!"

My dad wraps his arms around me, trying to get me to settle down. "Stella, calm down now."

"Honey, please," my mom says, grabbing my hand.

"Where is Will?" I cry out, but I can't see him anywhere. My eyes scan frantically, but my body gives up, falling weakly back onto the gurney.

All I can see is his body slouched over mine, all of his air given to me.

"Stella," I hear a weak voice say. "I'm here."

Will.

He's alive.

I turn my head toward the sound of the voice, my eyes finding his.

We can't be more than ten feet apart, but it feels farther than ever. I want to reach out, to touch him. To make sure he's okay.

"Take the lungs," he whispers, looking at me like I'm the only one here.

No. I can't. If I take the lungs, I will outlive him by close to a decade. If I take the lungs, he'll be more of a danger to me than ever. They won't let us in the same zip code, let alone room. And if I got B. cepacia after I got the healthy lungs all CFers want? It'd be wrong. It'd be devastating.

"You're taking the lungs, Stella," my mom says next to me, her hand tightening around my arm.

I look at my dad, grabbing his hand desperately. "Do you know how many things I am going to lose to CF? That I already have lost? The lungs won't change that."

I'm tired. I'm tired of fighting myself.

Everyone is quiet.

"I don't want to lose Will, though," I say, meaning it. "I love him, Dad."

I look from my dad to my mom, and then to Barb and Dr. Hamid. Willing them to understand.

"Take them. Please," Will says, and he struggles to climb out from under an emergency blanket, the skin on his chest and stomach and abdomen a pale blue color. His arms give way as Julie and a woman with his eyes push him back down.

"But if I do, it doesn't change anything for us, Will. It makes it worse," I say, knowing that new lungs won't rid me of cystic fibrosis.

"One step at a time," he says, holding my gaze. "This is your chance. And that is what we *both* want. Don't think about what you've lost. Think of how much you have to gain. Live, Stella."

I can feel Abby's arms around me back at the pond, holding me close. I can hear her voice in my ear, saying the same words that Will is saying now.

Live, Stella.

I take a deep breath and feel the familiar fight for air that I have every single day. When I was with Abby, I said I wanted to live. I'll have to worry about how after. "Okay," I say, nodding to Dr. Hamid, and the decision is made.

Relief fills Will's eyes, and he stretches out, placing his hand on a medical cart sitting between our gurneys. I reach out, putting my hand on the other side. There's stainless steel between us, but it doesn't matter.

His hand is still on the cart as I slowly start to roll away. To new lungs. To a new start.

But away from him.

I hear my parents' footsteps behind me, and Barb's, and Dr. Hamid's, but I look back at Will, one more time, his eyes meeting mine. And in that look I see him when we met the first time in the hallway, running his fingers through his hair. I see him holding the other end of the pool cue while we walk through the hospital, telling me to stick around for the next year. I see him cut through the water in the pool, the light dancing off his eyes. I see him across the table from me at his party, laughing until tears stream down his face.

I see the way he looked at me when he said that he loved me, only a few hours ago, on that icy pond.

I see him wanting to kiss me.

And now he smiles that lopsided smile from the day we first met, that familiar light filling his eyes, until he's out of view. But I still hear his voice. I still hear Abby's voice.

Live, Stella.

CHAPTER 28

WILL

I fall weakly back onto my gurney, my entire body aching. She's getting new lungs. *Stella is getting new lungs.* Through the pain, my heart thumps happily. My mom's hand wraps gently around my arm as Julie puts the oxygen mask over my face.

And then I remember.

No.

I sit bolt upright, my chest searing as I shout down the hallway. "Dr. Hamid!"

In the distance, she turns back to look at me, frowning, and nodding for Barb to follow her while the attending nurse keeps rolling Stella through into her surgery. I look at the both of them before I look down at my hands.

"I gave her mouth-to-mouth."

The room goes absolutely still as everyone processes what that means. She probably has B. cepacia. And it's all my fault.

"She wasn't breathing," I say, swallowing. "I had to. I'm so sorry."

I look up, into Barb's eyes, and then over at Dr. Hamid. "You did good, Will," she says, nodding at me, reassuring me. "You saved her *life*, okay? And if she contracted B. cepacia, we'll deal with it."

She looks at Barb, and then at Julie, and then back at me. "But if we don't use those lungs, they're wasted. We're doing the surgery."

They leave, and I slowly sink back onto the gurney, the weight of everything pressing down on my entire body. Exhaustion fills every part of me. I shiver, my rib cage aching from the cold. I meet my mom's eyes as Julie puts the O_2 mask back over my mouth, watching as my mom reaches out to gently stroke my hair like she did when I was younger.

I close my eyes, breathing in and out, and let the pain and the cold give way to sleep.

I glance at my watch. Four hours. It's been four hours since they took her back.

Shaking my leg nervously, I sit in the waiting room, staring anxiously out the window at the snow. I shiver despite myself, reliving the icy shock of the water from just a few hours ago. My mom kept trying to get me to go back to my room, put on more layers, but I want to be here. *Need* to be here. As close to Stella as I can be.

I pull my eyes away from the window, hearing footsteps coming steadily closer and closer. Looking over, I see Stella's mom sitting down in the chair two away from mine, a cup of coffee clutched in her hands.

"Thank you," she says finally, her eyes meeting mine. "For saving her life."

I nod, fixing my nose cannula, the oxygen hissing noisily out. "She wasn't breathing. Anyone would have—"

"I mean the lungs," she says, her eyes traveling to the window. "Her father and I, we just couldn't . . ." Her voice trails off, but I know what she's saying. She shakes her head, looking over at the clock hanging above the OR doors. "Just a few more hours."

I smile at her. "Don't worry. She'll be out making a 'Thirty-Eight-Step Lung-Transplant Recovery Plan' in no time."

She laughs, and a comfortable silence settles over the both of us until she goes off to get some lunch.

I sit alone, still nervous, alternating between texting Jason and Hope and staring at the wall, images of Stella swirling around my head, separate moments over the past few weeks jumping out at me.

I want to draw it all.

The first day we met, Stella in her makeshift hazmat suit, the birthday dinner. Each memory more precious than the next.

The elevator doors slide open, and Barb, as if she's heard

my thoughts, emerges carrying an armful of my art supplies.

"Staring at the wall can get a bit boring after a while," she says, handing everything off to me.

I laugh. Ain't that the truth.

"Any news?" I ask her, desperate to know how the surgery is going. But, more important, the results of the culture. I need to know I didn't give Stella B. cepacia. That those lungs will give her the time she wants.

Barb shakes her head. "Nothing yet." She glances over at the OR doors, taking a deep breath. "I'll tell you the second I hear something."

I open to the first blank page in my sketchbook and start to draw, the memories coming to life again in front of my eyes. Slowly, noon comes, the door busting open as Stella's parents come back, Camila and Mya trailing a few feet behind, cafeteria food containers piled high in everyone's hands.

"Will!" Mya says, running over to give me a one-arm hug, careful not to drop her food. I try not to wince, my body still weak from last night.

"We didn't know what you'd want, so we brought you a sandwich," Camila says as they all sit down in the chairs next to me, Stella's mom opening her purse to pull out a plastic-wrapped hoagie.

I smile gratefully, my stomach growling its appreciation. "Thank you."

Looking up from my drawing, I watch all of them as they eat, talking about what Stella will do now, their words overflowing with love for her. She's the glue that holds them all together. Her parents. Camila and Mya. Every single one of them needs her.

I pull my eyes away and draw, each page filled with another picture of our story.

The hours swim together—Camila and Mya leaving, Barb and Julie coming and going—but I keep drawing, wanting every little detail to be remembered forever. I look over at her parents, her mom fast asleep on her dad's chest, his arms wrapped protectively around her as his eyes slowly close.

I smile to myself. Seems like Stella isn't the only one to get a second chance today.

The OR doors swing open, and Dr. Hamid comes through with a small entourage of surgeons.

My eyes widen and I reach out, nudging her parents awake, and we all stand, studying their faces anxiously. Did she make it? Is she okay?

Dr. Hamid pulls down her surgical mask, smiling, and the three of us sigh with relief.

"Looks great," one of the surgeons says.

"Oh, thank god!" Stella's mom pulls her dad into a tight hug. I laugh with them, all of us elated. Stella made it.

Stella has new lungs.

• • •

I plunk down on my bed, absolutely worn out but happier than I've ever been. Looking up, I meet my mom's gaze as she sits in a chair next to my bed.

"Are you warm enough?" she asks me for the millionth time since she got back to the hospital. I look down at my two layers of sweatpants and three layers of shirts I put on to appease her, a smile creeping onto my face.

"I'm practically sweating at this point." I tug at the neck of my hoodie.

There's a knock and Barb peers around the door, meeting my eyes as she holds up a sheet full of test results. I'm paralyzed; her eyes aren't giving away anything of what I'm about to hear.

She pauses, leaning against the door as she scans the paper. "The bacterial cultures will take a few days to grow, and there's still a chance it will grow in her sputum. But as of now . . ." She smiles at me, shaking her head. "She's clean. She didn't get it. I don't know how in the hell, but she didn't."

Oh my god.

As of now, she's B. cepacia free.

As of now, that's enough.

"What about Will?" my mom asks from behind me. "The Cevaflomalin?"

I meet Barb's gaze, a look of understanding passing between us. She swallows, glancing back down at the papers in her hand, the results of a test I already know the answer to.

"It's not working for me, is it?" I ask.

She lets out a long sigh and shakes her head. "No. It's not."

Aw, shit.

I try not to look at my mom, but I can feel the distress on her face. The sadness. I reach out and take her hand, squeezing it gently. For the first time, I think I'm actually as disappointed as she is.

I look up at Barb remorsefully. "I'm so sorry for all of this."

She shakes her head and sighs. "No, sweetie . . ." She trails off, shrugging and smiling faintly at me. "Love is love."

Barb leaves and I hold my mom's hand while she cries, knowing she did all she could do. It's no one's fault.

She eventually falls asleep, and I sit in a chair by the window, watching as the sun slowly sets on the horizon. The lights at the park that Stella never got to see switching on as another day ends.

I wake up in the middle of the night, restless. Sliding into my shoes, I sneak out of my room, heading down to the first floor, to the recovery room where Stella sleeps. I watch her from the open door, her small body hooked up to large machines that do the job of breathing for her.

She made it.

I inhale, letting the air fill my lungs the best it can, the discomfort tugging at my chest, but I also feel relief.

Relief that Stella gets to wake up a few hours from now

and have at least five more wonderful years, filled with whatever her to-do list has on it. And maybe, if she's feeling fearless, a few things not on there, like going to see some holiday lights at one a.m.

When I exhale, though, I feel something else. A need to keep all those years safe.

I tighten my jaw, and even though everything in me wants to fight it, I know exactly what I have to do.

I look around the room at the small army I've assembled. Barb, Julie, Jason, Hope, Mya, Camila, Stella's parents. It's the most ragtag crew I've ever seen, standing there, staring at the boxes laid out on my bed, each of them with a separate but important role. I hold up my drawing, showing the intricate plan I spent most of the morning working on, every detail perfectly accounted for and coinciding with a different person and a task.

Stella would be proud.

I hear my mom's voice from the hallway, loud and firm and getting stuff done as she does her part.

I shiver, thinking about when she uses that tone on me.

"So," I say, looking up at all of them. "We have to do this together."

My eyes land on Hope, who wipes away a tear as Jason hugs her close. I look away, at Julie, at Camila and Mya, at Stella's parents.

"Is everyone in?"

Julie nods enthusiastically, and there's a chorus of agreement. Then everyone looks at Barb, who is dead silent.

"Oh, hell yes! I'm in. I'm definitely in," she says, smiling, the two of us on the same page for the first time probably ever.

"How long will Stella be sedated?" I ask her.

She glances down at her watch. "Probably a few more hours." Her eyes scan all the boxes, the list of each of our tasks. "We've got *plenty* of time."

Perfect.

I start handing out the boxes, pairing each person with their job. "All right, Camila and Mya," I say, giving them their task list and joint box. "You two are going to be working with Jason and Hope on the—"

My mom ends her call, poking her head back in the room. "It's done. They said yes."

YES! I knew she could do it. I shake my head. "You really are scary sometimes, you know that?"

She smiles back at me. "I've had some good practice."

I hand out the rest of the boxes, and everyone heads out into the hallway to start getting everything ready. My mom lingers back, peeking her head inside the doorway. "You need anything?"

I shake my head. "I'll be there soon. There's just one more thing I need to do first."

The door closes, and I turn to my desk, pulling on a pair of latex gloves and taking out my colored pencils. I've been stuck on the same drawing. A drawing of Stella, spinning around on that icy pond, moments before I told her I loved her.

I keep trying to get every small detail right. The moonlight shining off her face. Her hair trailing behind her as she spins. Pure joy filling every feature.

Tears fill my eyes as I stare at the drawing, and I brush them away with my arm, knowing that for once, I'm doing the absolute right thing.

I stand in Stella's doorway again, watching the steady rise and fall of her bandaged chest, her new lungs working perfectly. The now-dry panda is tucked safely under her arm, her face peaceful as she sleeps.

I love her.

I used to always be searching for *something*. Searching from every rooftop for something that would give me a purpose.

And now I've found it.

"She's waking up," her dad says as Stella begins to stir.

I look up as her mom crosses the room, her eyes beginning to water as she looks at me. "Thank you, Will."

I nod as I reach into my bag with a gloved hand and pull out a wrapped package. "Give this to her when she wakes up?"

Her mom takes it and gives me a small, sad smile.

Then I look at Stella one more time as her eyelids start to

flutter. I want to stay. I want to stay in that doorway, and right by her side. Even if it's always five feet away.

Six feet, even.

But for exactly that reason, I exhale, and with everything in me, I turn and walk away.

CHAPTER 29

STELLA

I open my eyes.

I stare at the ceiling, everything coming into focus, the pain from the surgery radiating across my entire body.

Will.

I try to look around, but I'm too weak. There's people here, but I don't see him. I try to speak but can't because of the ventilator.

My eyes land on my mother's face and she holds up a package. "Honey?" my mom whispers, holding it out to me. "This is for you."

A present? That's odd.

I struggle to rip open the paper, but my body is weak. She leans over to help me unveil a black sketchbook inside, the words on the front reading "FIVE FEET APART."

It's from Will.

I flip through the pages, looking at cartoon after cartoon

of our story, the colors jumping out at me. Me holding the panda, the two of us standing on either side of the pool cue, us floating underwater, the filled table at his birthday party, me spinning around and around on the icy pond.

Then, on the last page, the two of us. In my small cartoon hand is a balloon, the top bursting, and hundreds of stars pouring out of it, rolling across the page to Will.

He's holding a scroll and quill, the words "Will's Master List" written on it.

And below, a single item.

"#1: Love Stella Forever."

I smile and look around at all the faces in the room. Then why isn't he here?

Julie takes a step forward, propping an iPad up on my lap. I frown, confused.

She presses play.

"My beautiful, bossy Stella," Will says, his face appearing on the screen, his hair its usual charming mess, his smile as lopsided as ever.

"I guess it's true what that book of yours says—the soul knows no time. These past few weeks will last forever for me." He takes a deep breath, smiling with those blue eyes. "My only regret is that you never got to see your lights."

I look up, surprised, as the lights in my room suddenly go out. I see Julie standing by the switch.

Suddenly the courtyard outside my recovery room window is ablaze, the entire space filled with the twinkling holiday lights from the park, twisting around the lampposts and the trees. I gasp as they cast a glow into my room. Barb and Julie unlock the bed, rolling it right up to the window so I can see.

And there, on the other side of the glass, standing under a canopy of those beautiful lights, is Will.

My eyes widen as I realize what's happening.

He's leaving. Will's leaving. I grip at the sheets as a different kind of pain takes over.

He smiles at me, looking down and pulling out his phone. Behind me, my phone starts ringing. Julie brings it to me, putting it on speaker. I open my mouth to speak, to say something, to tell him to *stay*, but nothing comes out.

The ventilator tube hisses.

I try to somehow tell him through my look not to leave. That I need him.

He gives me a faint smile, and I see the tears in his blue eyes. "Finally, I've got you speechless," he says, his voice pouring out of the phone.

He raises his hand, putting it up against the glass of the window. I weakly raise mine, resting it on top of his, the glass just the latest thing keeping us apart.

I want to scream.

Stay.

"People in the movies are always saying, 'You have to love

someone enough to let them go.'" He shakes his head, swallowing, struggling to speak. "I always thought that was such bullshit. But seeing you almost die . . ."

His voice trails off, and my fingers curl against the cool window, wanting to smash it, but I can barely manage a knock. "In that moment nothing else mattered to me. Nothing. Except your life."

He presses harder too, his voice shaking as he continues. "The only thing I want is to be with you. But I *need* for you to be safe. Safe from *me*."

He fights to continue, tears streaming down his face. "I don't want to leave you, but I love you too much to stay." He laughs through his tears, shaking his head. "God, the freakin' movies were right."

He leans his head against the window where my hand rests. I can feel it, even through the glass. I can feel him.

"I will love you forever," he says, looking up so we're face-to-face, the both of us silently seeing the same pain in each other's eyes. My heart slowly cracks under the new scar.

My breath fogs up the glass, and one more time I lift a shaking finger, drawing a heart.

"Will you please close your eyes?" he asks, his voice breaking. "I'm not gonna be able to walk away from you if you're looking at me."

But I refuse. He looks up, seeing the defiance in my face. But the certainty in his surprises me.

"Don't worry about me," he says, smiling through the tears. "If I stop breathing tomorrow, know that I wouldn't change a thing."

I love him. And he's about to leave my life forever so that I can have a life to live.

"Please close your eyes," he begs, his jaw tightening. "Let me go."

I take a moment to memorize his face, every inch of it, and finally I force my eyes shut as sobs rack my body, fighting with the ventilator.

He's leaving.

Will's leaving.

When I open my eyes, he will be *gone.*

Tears stream down my face as I feel him walk away, much farther than the five feet that we agreed on. That was always between us.

I open my eyes slowly, some part of me still hoping he'll be on the other side of the glass. But all I see are the twinkling lights in the courtyard and a town car in the distance, disappearing into the night.

My fingertips reach up, shaking, as I touch his lip print on the window. His final kiss good-bye.

EIGHT MONTHS LATER

CHAPTER 30

WILL

The speaker in the airport terminal crackles to life, a muffled voice breaking through the morning chatter and the suitcase wheels clunking over the tiled floor. I pull out one of my earbuds to hear the voice, worried about a gate change and having to go cross-airport with a pair of shitty lungs. "Your attention please, passengers for Icelandair flight 616 to Stockholm . . ."

I put my earbud back in. Not my flight. I'm not going to Sweden until December.

Settling back into the armchair, I pull up YouTube for the millionth time, making my way as usual to Stella's last video. If YouTube kept track of individual views, the police definitely would have been sent to my house by now, I'd seem like such a stalker. But I don't care, because this video is about us. And when I press play, she tells our story.

"Human touch. Our first form of communication," she

says, her voice loud and clear. She takes a deep breath, her new lungs working wonderfully.

That breath is my favorite part of the whole video. There's no struggle. No wheezing. It's perfect and smooth. Effortless.

"Safety, security, comfort, all in the gentle caress of a finger, or the brush of lips on a soft cheek," she says, and I look up from my iPad to the crowded airport around me, people coming and going, heavy bags in tow, but even so, she's right. From the long hugs at arrival, to the reassuring hands on shoulders in the security line, even a young couple, arms around each other, waiting at the gate, touch is everywhere.

"We need that touch from the one we love, almost as much as we need air to breathe. I never understood the importance of touch, his touch . . . until I couldn't have it."

I can see her. Five feet away from me, that night at the pool, walking to see the lights, on the other side of the glass that last night, always that longing between us to close the gap.

I pause the video just to take her in.

She looks . . . so much better than I ever saw her in person. No portable oxygen. No dark circles under her eyes.

She was always beautiful to me, but now she is *free.* She is *alive.*

Every single day I still find myself wishing I hadn't left, reliving the moment of walking away, my legs like cement blocks, being pulled like a magnet back to her window. I think that pull, that hurt, will always be there. But all I have to do is see her like this to know it was worth it a million times over.

A notification appears on my screen from her app, telling me to take my midmorning meds. I smile at the dancing pill bottle emoji. It's like a portable Stella that I always have with me, looking over my shoulder, reminding me to do my treatments. Reminding me of the importance of more time.

"You ready to go, man?" Jason says, nudging me as they open the door to start loading the plane to Brazil. I give him a big smile, down my meds dry, and slide my pillbox back into my backpack, zipping it up.

"Born ready."

I'm finally going to *see* the places I've dreamed of.

I have a checkup in every city, which was one of three conditions my mom put in place before letting me go. The other two were simple. I have to send her as many pictures as possible, and Skype her every Monday evening, no matter what. Aside from that, I can finally live my life how I want. And, for once, that includes fighting right alongside her.

We've finally found common ground.

I stand, taking a deep breath as I pull the strap of my portable oxygen farther up on my thin shoulder. But the breath gets caught in my throat almost as soon as I inhale. Because through all the airport chatter and chaos, just above the rattling of the mucus in my lungs, I hear my favorite sound in the world.

Her laugh. It tinkles like bells, and I pull out my phone immediately, certain I've left the video playing in my pocket. But the screen is dark, and the sound isn't tinny or distant.

It's just a few feet away.

My legs know I should just go, board my flight, keep moving. But my eyes are already searching. I have to know.

It takes me about six seconds to spot her, and I'm not even surprised that when I do, her eyes are right on mine.

Stella was always the one to find me first.

CHAPTER 31

STELLA

"What happened to winging it, Stella? Doing it 'Abby Style,'" Mya says, nudging me playfully.

I glance up from my itinerary, laughing as I carefully fold it and put it into my back pocket. "Rome wasn't built in a day." I smirk at her and Camila, proud of my Vatican City joke. "Get it? Rome?"

Camila laughs, rolling her eyes. "New lungs, but not a new sense of humor."

I take a deep breath at her words, my lungs effortlessly expanding and contracting. It's still so wonderful, I can hardly believe it. These past eight months have been bittersweet, to say the least. My new lungs are amazing, the physical pain of the surgery gradually giving way to a whole new life. My parents are back together, and we're all finally starting to mend, too. Like my new lungs, it hasn't fixed everything that's broken. The losses of Abby and Poe are pains I don't think I'll ever fully get over. Just like I know that no matter what, some part of me will never get over Will. And that's okay.

The pain reminds me that they were here, that I'm alive.

Thanks to Will I have so much more life to live. So much more *time.* Aside from his love, it was the greatest gift I could ever receive. And I can't believe now that I almost didn't take it.

I gaze around the airport at the high ceilings and the wide windows, excitement coursing through my veins as we walk to gate 17 for our flight to Rome. A trip I can finally take. To Vatican City and the Sistine Chapel and the first of so many things I want to do and see. It isn't with Abby, and I certainly won't be crossing off that one item on Will's bucket list, but just going makes me feel closer to them.

I realize as we walk that I'm setting the pace, Camila and Mya following right behind. I would have keeled over from this much walking a few months ago, but now it feels like I could just keep going.

"Everyone in for a picture!" Mya says when we find our gate, holding up her phone as we squeeze together, smiling big for the camera.

After the flash we pull apart and I glance down at my phone to see a picture from my mom of my dad eating breakfast, his eggs and bacon in the shape of a sad face with the caption MISS YOU ALREADY, STELL! Send pictures!

I laugh, nudging Mya. "Hey, make sure you send it to my

parents; they've already been asking nonstop for pictures of . . ."

My voice trails off as I see that her mouth is open in shock, and she's staring at Camila.

"What? Did I do that thing with my face again?" Camila asks, sighing loudly. "I don't know why I keep smiling like that—"

Mya holds up her hand to cut her off, her eyes flicking urgently to a big group of people waiting to board their plane, finally focusing on something behind me. Camila inhales sharply.

I turn around, following her gaze, the hairs on the back of my neck standing on end as my eyes travel down the long line of people.

My heart begins to beat faster when my eyes land on Jason.

And then I know. I know he's there even before I see him.

Will.

I stand, frozen in place as he looks up and our eyes lock, the familiar blue that I've dreamed about for so long almost knocking me off my feet. He's still sick, portable oxygen slung over his shoulder, his face gaunt and tired. It's almost a physical pain to see him like this, to feel my lungs filling anew when his can't.

But then his mouth turns up into that lopsided smile and the world melts away. It's Will. It's really him. He's sick, but alive. We both are.

I take a deep, unhindered breath and walk over to him, stopping exactly six feet away from him. His eyes are warm as he takes me in. No portable oxygen, no difficulty breathing, no nose cannula.

I'm practically a different Stella.

Except for one thing.

I smile at him, and take just that one more stolen step, until we're five feet apart.

AUTHORS' NOTE

The drug Cevaflomalin that Will participates in a trial for is a fictional creation. We hope that one day such a treatment is found.

ACKNOWLEDGMENTS

Rachael

First and foremost, this book is for the thousands of individuals around the world with cystic fibrosis. I hope with all my heart that it will raise awareness for CF and will help each and every one of you feel heard.

Thank you to Mikki Daughtry and Tobias Iaconis for trusting me with your beautiful screenplay and the story of Will and Stella. It was an honor to be able to work with the two of you.

I am extremely grateful to Simon & Schuster for the opportunity, and my amazing editor, Alexa Pastor, who is absolutely brilliant at what she does.

Huge thanks to my agent, Rachel Ekstrom Courage, at Folio Literary Management for all her help.

Also to the most wonderful of mentors, Siobhan Vivian.

To my best friend, Lianna Rana, the Monday Night Trivia Crew of Larry Law, Alyssa Zolkiewicz, Kyle Richter, and Kat Loh, and to Judy Derrick: Your abundance of support and love has been overwhelming. I couldn't have done this without you.

Special thanks to my mom, who has believed in me since the day I was born. You simply redefine what it means to be a single parent, and I am eternally grateful for your strength and bravery and care through the years.

And, finally, to my love, Alyson Derrick. Thank you, thank you, thank you for being exactly who you are. You are light itself.

Mikki & Tobias

This story is dedicated to Claire Wineland and to all the CFers who still bravely fight the battle against cystic fibrosis. Claire's courage and perseverance in the face of her lifelong illness should be a lesson to us all. Keep fighting, keep smiling, keep calm. We knew her for but a short time, yet her influence on our lives will continue for the rest of our days. Her contributions to this story were immense. Her contributions to the story of humanity were, and will forever be, endless.

To Justin Baldoni, who never takes "no" for an answer. Justin's dedication, drive, and compassion have inspired us in every way. His unwavering vision for this project taught us that with talent, focus, and ambition, great things can happen. We thank him from the bottom of our hearts.

To Cathy Schulman, whose twenty-four-hour on-call presence was never more needed than at three a.m. Cathy's knowledge, experience, and creative wisdom elevated every page, every scene. It was an honor and a joy to watch her work. And she let us hold her Oscar. Now THAT was a thrill!

To Terry Press, Mark Ross, Sean Ursani, and the entire CBS Films team. We count ourselves so very fortunate for their guiding hands at every turn. None of this would have been possible without their faith in this project. We got to work with a true dream team and each day we felt blessed beyond belief.

And to Rachael Lippincott, whose Herculean efforts to

novelize this story were amazing to watch and even more amazing to read. Thank you, thank you, thank you!

Without the tireless efforts of everyone involved, there would be no screenplay. There would be no movie. There would be no book. For all of this, we are forever grateful.